TOM SWIFT®
2
TERROR ON THE
MOONS OF JUPITER

"Give it everything we have!" Tom said,
making no attempt to hide the urgency in
his voice. The view out the ports had
become hazy, as if they were entering a
great orange cloud. They had penetrated
the atmosphere of Jupiter!

The cloud thickened into an orange fog and
almost simultaneously the ship began to
quiver. The shakes became bucks as the
ship fought the gravity and turbulence of
the Great Red Spot's eternal storms. Tom
realised Foster had lost orientation as he
fired the attitude jets that pushed the ship
inward, not outward. The ship screamed as
the tortured metal was bent...

"We're going through the Great Red Spot!
It's a gigantic storm..."

TOM SWIFT®
2
TERROR ON THE
MOONS OF JUPITER
by Victor Appleton

A CAROUSEL BOOK

TRANSWORLD PUBLISHERS LTD.

Other TOM SWIFT® books:

No. 1: THE CITY IN THE STARS

No. 3: THE ALIEN PROBE

No. 4: THE WAR IN OUTER SPACE

published by Carousel Books

TOM SWIFT®: TERROR ON THE MOONS
OF JUPITER

A CAROUSEL BOOK   0   552   52155   8

First published in Great Britain in 1981

PRINTING HISTORY
Carousel edition published 1981

Carousel Books are published by
Transworld Publishers Ltd.,
Century House, 61–63 Uxbridge Road,
Ealing, London W5 5SA.

Made and printed in the United States of America by
Arcata Graphics, Buffalo, New York.

TOM SWIFT®
2
TERROR ON THE
MOONS OF JUPITER

CHAPTER ONE

"Hit the deck," Tom yelled. He tucked his lofty frame into a compact ball and rolled backwards. He came out of the roll in a balanced crouch as the massive, "skinless", multi-jointed arm of the robot whizzed past him, exactly where his rib cage had been moments before.

Ben Walking Eagle and Anita Thorwald reacted instantly to Tom's warning. They fell straight to the floor from the balls of their feet, cushioning the impact with their lower arms and the palms of their hands, and yelled, "EEEE" to expel the air from their lungs.

They looked up just in time to see the robot's arm rip through the heavy steel bulkhead, then stop, its naked struts and wires caught in the jagged edges and broken wires of the hole it had just torn in the lab of the space ship *Daniel Boone*.

"Stop program," Tom shouted at the squat mechanoid. "Shut down for reprogramming!"

There was a whirring sound and then Tom, Ben and Anita heard the squish of traction pads on the deck. The robot's mainframe and motorframe rotated ninety degrees, then jerked to a stop. All of its sections now faced forward, except for the pinned arm.

"At least the EXCOM circuit is working," Anita remarked dryly. The supple redhead stood up and brushed at the knees of her white jumpsuit which were now dirty. Tom winced at the criticism in her remark.

The robot's EXCOM—or EXterior COMmunications circuit—translated human speech into binary numbers by using pitch, rather than actual consonant and vowel sounds, as reference. EXCOM made vocal command possible by exactly identifying human vocal frequencies and translating them in terms of cycles per second.

Tom's emotions were mixed, as he turned his attention to the robot. A spaceship, on its way to Jupiter, was no place for an accident. They had been lucky. He had designed the robot for conditions in space and on high and low gravity planets, and he had used the latest technology and materials that were available. His family's giant multimillion-dollar scientific-industrial complex, Swift Enterprises, had made it possible. His own inventive genius, inherited from his father, Tom Swift, Senior, had made it a reality. The end product of months of planning, design, and construction stood before him, compact, massive, mobile, semi-intelligent...and deadly?

If Ben or Anita—or even he, Tom—had been hurt badly, emergency medical treatment would have been limited to what was available on the *Daniel Boone*. True, the ship's medical facilities were the best possible, under the circumstances, but it wasn't like having an entire hospital, Earth-side.

And what about the *Daniel Boone*, itself, Tom thought. The giant ship, constructed in space for the exploration of the solar system, couldn't be "garaged" every time something went wrong or got broken.

Accidents always offended Tom's sense of order, but this one had scared him more than he wanted to admit.

Tom tried to break his train of thought, glancing up at the robot's "face". At the moment, the sensorframe was incomplete and only the sonar transducers were in place. They were the robot's only means of "seeing", for the time being. By emitting ultrasonic beams in all directions and "listening" for the echoes, the robot sensed its distance from objects and could avoid bumping into things, now that it was operational. When complete, the robot would have other kinds of sight, as well. TV cameras, and photosensitive arrays would also be part of the robot's sensor system, allowing it to see in several different ways depending on the conditions. Sonarscan, however, would always have the advantage of requiring the least amount of power.

"Poor, dumb, half-blind machine," Tom said out loud.

"You talk as if you actually feel sorry for it," Ben said, peering over Tom's shoulder at the silent, motionless robot.

"I do."

"Ah, Herr Doctor Frankenstein," quipped Anita, "you have created a monster!"

Ben patted the metal shoulder of the robot protectively. "Shhhhh! You'll hurt his feelings!"

"I forgot that he's still—'on'! Can he hear what we're saying?"

"I doubt it, although when I gave him the 'shut down for reprogramming' instruction, it only locked his servodrive in the forward position."

Tom rummaged through his tool box and then withdrew a tool which resembled a screwdriver with a pointed tip. It had a black wire coming out of the handle with an alligator clip on the end. The handle had a place for a digital readout.

The young inventor peered into the mass of interwoven wires and hydraulic lines in the robot's shoulder and, a moment later, carefully selected a red wire. He clipped the tool's "pigtail" onto the robot's mainframe, and then stabbed through the red wire's insulation with the pointed end. He touched the digital readout for a moment, then nodded in satisfaction.

"Now that the robot's nuclear cells are operational, he can't be *totally* shut down except by special equipment," he said. "I've got continuity, so the arm is intact."

Anita looked at the robot uncertainly. Outwardly, it remained motionless and silent. The only sign of life was a tiny glowing light on the sensorframe. Her gaze fell on the robot's injured arm. "Uh, oh, we've got a problem, Tom," she

10

said, bending closer to the robot's wrist. "Look at this!"

Anita pointed to the bulkhead and Tom groaned as he watched a small drop of oily fluid dribble down the smooth metal surface.

"The metal of the bulkhead must have cut through a hydraulic line," he said. "It's a good thing you spotted that fluid, Anita, because that line would never have held pressure. We would have had a real mess on our hands if that stuff had started squirting out under load!"

For all its electronic complexity, the robot was really a very simple mechanism in many ways. For sheer operating efficiency, power, and speed of response Tom had chosen to go with electrohydraulics, a very basic system, that functioned on the principle that an oil in a confined space cannot be compressed. When pressure is applied to any part of it, that pressure is transferred throughout the oil with no loss of energy.

The robot had electrically activated hydraulic cylinders located at all of its movement points. An electronic signal given by the central processing unit for a specific movement activated a piston inside the hydraulic cylinder. The piston put pressure on the hydraulic fluid—the oil—and that pressure was transferred throughout the line. The robot's movement was only limited by the sensitivity of the pressure sensors, and Tom had worked very hard to make them as sensitive as possible.

"There's a pinhole rupture in the green line," Tom said, peering closely at the robot's damaged arm. "We'll have to heat-seal it so that the line will hold pressure until we can replace it."

11

"I'll do it," said Ben. The young computer tech went to a metal cabinet and returned with a tool that looked like some sort of science fiction ray gun. It was actually a small laser. Ben held a tiny piece of patching plastic with a pair of forceps and heated it with the laser. Then he placed the heated plastic over the pinhole and held the laser on it for a few seconds until it fused with the hydraulic line.

"We'd better get to work and untangle that arm now," said Anita. "He must be pretty bored standing there like that!"

For the next two hours, Tom, Ben and Anita painstakingly untangled the robot's arm from the mass of broken wires and jagged metal of the bulkhead. They had to be extremely careful not to pull any of its wires from the various pressure pickups and attitude sensors located throughout the arm. Once all of the testing was completed on the robot's arms, they would be sheathed in metal to protect the delicate inner circuitry from any environment. Articulation rings at the joints would permit the arms to bend in an almost human way.

"It makes you appreciate the complexity of the human body," Ben said. He was carefully extracting a wire from the robot's "wrist" with a pair of long, thin tweezers. "Until we started working on this robot, I never realized how complicated even a simple movement, like picking up a water glass, is. It probably takes billions of nerve impulses from our brains just to hold the glass, without breaking it! You're a wiring genius, Tom Swift!"

"And I had no idea how many 'thought steps' have to go into programming a computer in order to make a program work, until you explained it to me, Ben," Tom said. He smiled up at his friend, and laughed when he saw Ben blushing at the unexpected compliment.

"There's nothing special about…"

"There he goes with the modesty routine again," Anita broke in. "If it hadn't been for you, Benjamin Franklin Walking Eagle, computer circuit tracker, par excellence, the *Daniel Boone* would be so much space garbage and we would all be 'one with the universe' in a way that I don't care to think about!"

"Wait a minute…"

"I agree with Anita," Tom said. "If you hadn't tracked down Doctor Grotz's computer file on the defective space drive he was going to put in the *Daniel Boone*, we wouldn't be on our way to Jupiter right now!"

"Well, it *is* in the genes, I suppose," the young computer tech said, jokingly, referring to his American Indian heritage.

"I liked the modesty routine better, I think," Anita teased.

A few minutes later, Tom extracted the last broken wire from the robot's arm.

"Until we know what went wrong with the robot, I don't think you should give him any complicated instructions," Ben cautioned.

"The trouble is, I know *I* can't move that arm," Tom said, worriedly. "I don't think the three of us together can move it *or* the robot!"

Anita and Ben nodded their heads "yes" in silent agreement. The rip in the bulkhead spoke for itself. The robot was just too heavy to be pushed around like a piece of furniture.

Tom had known from the beginning that weight and manoeuvrability would be as important to the design of his robot as its brain. A robot that could not fit through the door of a spaceship, or a human habitation, or be transported wherever man had need of it, was of no use. He also knew that his robot would have to withstand and *survive* the worst conditions man and machine had ever faced before. A balance had to be achieved without sacrificing too much durability or too much efficiency.

Part of the weight problem had been solved back on Earth, at the Swift Enterprises Shopton, New Mexico main complex. Tom had used the corporation's giant Langley computer to formulate a new, light-weight, triple strength steel, which he called TSJ93000X. The first three letters in the designation were his initials. That indicated that he had formulated it. The "9" meant that the steel was a "high strength low alloy" (HSLA) steel. The "3000" was the stress strength in thousands of kilos per square centimetre. The "X" denoted that it was a micro-alloyed steel which contained about 0.1 percent of other metals such as vanadium, columbium, titanium, and zirconium as strengthening agents. Tom had used as much of the new steel as possible in the construction of the robot, but it still weighed a lot! The mindboggling thing was, that it took many kilometres of wiring, a half tonne of steel, and a sensorframe that weighed almost ninety kilogrammes to duplicate some of the functions of the human body with a third of the efficiency!

Tom's expression brightened, suddenly. "I just thought of something! If Anita doesn't mind, we can use her computer to by-pass the robot's central programming unit!"

"You mean use her computer as the robot's brain?" asked Ben. "I think it could be done. That way, we can get the robot to move *itself* to the big computer terminal they have over in the engineering section."

"Once it's there, we can do a circuit check and run the complete program to see what made the robot go berserk, like that! What do you say, Anita?" Tom asked. He looked at the beautiful redhead steadily. He did not want her to think she was being pressured into volunteering for anything she did not want to do, and he knew how sensitive she was, at times, about the computer, housed in her right leg, which was artificial just below the knee.

To his relief, Anita smiled and rolled up the leg of her jumpsuit, exposing the computer. All the circuits were visible through the clear plastic outer covering. Shaped to resemble a human leg, the outer covering was not a hard brittle plastic, but was, instead, made of a very thin layer of clear gel sandwiched between two pieces of pliable, high density clear plastic. It helped to cushion the shock of movement and it protected the computer's mainframe from impact—especially with chairs, table legs, and other objects in the human environment.

Anita's link with the computer, was a large bracelet on her right wrist. It contained a microterminal with an LED crystal face, and a surrounding display of buttons in various colours. The wrist controller was connected by a microscopically thin wire that ran through Anita's arm, down her side,

15

and through the main artery in her right leg to the computer.

The young woman held her wrist out and looked at her two friends questioningly. "Who's going to do the honours? I'm afraid this idea is a bit beyond my programming capabilities."

"Why don't you take care of that, while I do the wiring, Ben," said Tom. "I want to do this with a series hookup instead of by radio. That way, nothing can go wrong."

Ben sat down next to Anita and took her wrist, gently. "What should we call this program?" he asked.

"How about calling it 'a program to move the robot', and getting on with it, Ben," Anita said, sarcastically.

"You have no sense of humour," said Ben. However, he began punching buttons on the wrist controller, humming softly to himself.

An hour later, they were ready.

"The robot won't be able to boogie, but it will move, as long as Anita's computer is in control," said Ben. "There was no time to do a really detailed program."

"You two make a beautiful couple, Anita," said Tom. "Have you set the wedding date yet?" He barely had enough time to dodge as the volatile redhead swung at him with her left hand. She stood next to the large silent robot and was connected to it by a heavy gauge metre-long adaptor cable, which Tom had rigged to go from her wrist controller, to the robot's sensorframe.

"We'll take it *very* slow because we don't have EXCOM," said Tom. Anita looked at him nervously, but made no comment. "Luckily, there aren't a lot of turns to make once we get out of the lab. The turns will be the hardest manoeuvres. Is everybody ready?"

Ben and Anita nodded. Tom walked across the room to the hatch, and pressed the control. The pneumatic door hissed softly and began sliding open. "Activate him," said Tom. He watched, tensely, as Ben punched out the signal on Anita's wrist controller.

CHAPTER TWO

There was a sharp, loud popping sound and then an electric crackle. The robot jerked spasmodically and then a giant blue-white spark jumped from its wrist to a nearby dangling bulkhead wire. The insulation on the wire bubbled for a moment.

The robot jerked again and this time, Anita screamed as current arced from the robot's arm to the bulkhead wire.

"Abort," yelled Tom, and he saw Ben grab for Anita's wrist controller.

Suddenly, a thin stream of hydraulic fluid shot out from the robot's wrist and splashed on the bulkhead.

"It's from the blue line," shouted Ben. "I didn't see any fluid leaking from that one!"

Another spark shot from the robot's wrist to the bulkhead and the hydraulic fluid exploded into flame. Ben was driven back by the heat of the fire, and Tom saw Anita fall to her knees.

The room was filling rapidly with thick, blue-green smoke as the hydraulic fluid fed the electrical fire. Tom was barely able to see Anita as he rushed to her side. He could see that she was frightened, but in control of herself. He reached for her wrist controller, but the young woman wrenched her arm away.

"There's no time for that," she yelled, and wrapping the adaptor cord around her fist, she jerked it as hard as she could.

"No," yelled Tom. "Don't do that, Anita!" He tried to get the cord out of her hands but Anita seemed to possess super human strength. A tongue of flame shot out of the bulkhead, as the insulation on the electrical wires fed the fire. Tom put his arm across his eyes to protect them from the severe heat and he caught a glimpse of Anita using the massive robot as a shield.

Tom could hear Ben coughing from somewhere in the room, but the thick, toxic smoke prevented him from seeing if his friend was badly hurt.

Tom staggered dizzily back to Anita's side and grabbed for her wrist again. This time, however, he was off balance and the redhead gave him a mighty shove which sent him to the deck.

What happened next seemed, to Tom, like a slow-motion, haze-enveloped nightmare ballet. He saw Anita brace her good leg against the robot and pull the adaptor cord with all of her strength. He saw the cord stretch, and then it popped free of the rubber connector boot. The robot jerked once more, and was still.

The adaptor cable was still wrapped around Anita's hands and Tom could see sparks coming from the filaments on the broken end as she fell backward, away from the robot. But something was wrong with her, Tom's smoke-fogged mind told him. She looked like a rag doll that had been tossed out a window. He opened his mouth to call out to her but he could only choke as the thick, hot smoke poured down his throat. He saw her fall to the deck and lie there, unmoving.

Tom knew if he did not get air soon, he would collapse and if that happened, he and his two friends would die. He knew Ben was still alive because he could hear him gasping for air just as he was. Anita lay face down on the deck, but Tom could see she was not dead, only hurt very badly.

Air. He needed air and the fire was taking it all. Tom put his face against the deck and took shallow breaths. As long as he had air, he could stay conscious and live…as long as the fire had air, it would continue to burn. How could he cut off air to the fire?

"Must get Ben and Anita out," Tom gasped out loud. He would have to talk himself all the way through it. "Ben," he yelled. His throat felt raw from the heat and smoke. The sound was more of a gurgle than anything else.

The answer was a deep coughing to his left.

Tom stayed as low to the deck as he could. Slowly, he crawled in the direction of the sound. It seemed to take a long time just to move a metre or so. "Left hand out. Pull. Right hand out. Pull."

The outline of Ben's body appeared through the smoke. The young Indian was struggling to rise.

"Easy, Ben," Tom said. He grasped his friend's shoulder and shook it, weakly.

"Tom..."

"We have to get Anita out! I need your help!"

"How...?"

"Follow me."

Everything seemed to be taking a long time, but Tom knew that not more than four or five minutes could have passed since the first explosion. Time had been compressed that much.

Tom and Ben crawled toward a splotch of bright light that flickered hazily through the thick smoke. Anita should be there, he thought.

She was. Both boys could feel their strength leaving them. There wasn't much time left. The fire was spreading rapidly to the lab furniture. Soon, it would find new fuel inside the cupboards and on the shelves of the work area. Tom couldn't predict what would happen then.

The immediate problem was, that Anita, being unconscious, was a dead weight. Tom could barely drag his own body across the floor and now he had Anita to move, as well.

As carefully as he could, Tom grasped Anita's arm, near the shoulder, with one hand. With the other he took a firm hold on her jumpsuit near the waist. Ben did the same.

They pulled, then stopped, choking and gasping for air. They pulled, and rested. It was agonizingly slow, but somehow, an eternity later, they were through the lab door and into the corridor. It wasn't much of an improvement.

Ben fainted. Tom was near to fainting, himself, when, through the fog of semi-consciousness, he heard the sound of running footsteps.

A second later, he heard muffled voices shouting words that were vaguely recognizable and he felt strong hands grab hold of him.

The robot! He had forgotten all about it. He struggled to break free of the hands. More hands grabbed him. He tried to explain about the robot, but the hands weren't paying any attention.

He searched inside of himself, and found the last of his strength. He wrenched free of the hands, and lurched against the lab door.

". . . seal off . . . robot," he managed to croak.

He felt the press of bodies close to him. The door began to close. Someone shoved an oxygen mask over his face. At first it threatened to smother him, but he gasped, and involuntarily swallowed the life-giving air. He took more breaths, greedily gulping it in. His head began to clear. He was aware of more than just the hands now. He saw the faces of the emergency crew, through their oxygen masks. He saw the worry.

"Evacuate the chamber," Tom shouted. The words sounded alien, distorted, as they were, by the oxygen mask. The emergency crew seemed confused. Nobody moved.

Quickly, Tom reached for the handle of a small door fitted into the bulkhead and jerked it open. Reaching in, he grasped a large red handle. But he didn't pull it down immediately. Tendrils of the thick smoke were curling out from the edges of the lab door. It was not closed all the way, then.

"Help me seal the chamber," Tom said. He put all of his weight against the heavy steel door and heard the hinges whine. Two members of the crew followed his example, and the three of them put all their weight against the door. A fourth crewman spun the locking wheel.

Tom did not hesitate a moment after that. He reached for the handle and pulled it all the way down.

A compressor chugged to life from somewhere, nearby. That was it. The fire would be out within moments as all the air was sucked from the sealed lab. That was one of the safety features of the *Daniel Boone*. A vacuum could be created in any part of the giant ship, and all chambers could be sealed off from one another.

Tom sagged against the door, exhausted. He examined himself for the first time and saw that his clothing was torn and sooty. His hands stung and blisters were beginning to appear on them. He hadn't been aware of it, before. He felt the last bit of energy drain from his body, and he looked into the anxious faces of the emergency crew. He was embarrassed for being caught so helpless and so weak. The five gas-masked faces looked back at him. They seemed detached and alien-looking. Only the eyes were visible. Tom blinked. Five human beings with grotesque elephant snouts.

He laughed to himself. It was comical.

His knees buckled.

He let himself fall. The release felt good.

He sank gratefully into darkness.

Into oblivion.

CHAPTER THREE

"Dad?"

"Welcome back to the world, son."

Tom's eyes fluttered open. It was amazing how he had sensed his father, even before seeing him. It was like being in the presence of a...*presence*. But then, Tom Swift, Senior, had that effect on a lot of people. It was not in what he said or did. It was in what he *was*. His character had been forged in the years of building a small back yard business into a multi-national scientific-industrial complex. At forty-nine, the elder Swift had lost none of his creative genius and dynamic force of will.

Tom's vision came into focus and he saw that he was in the ship's infirmary, rather than in his own quarters.

"We wanted to make sure you had no internal injuries, Tom," his father said. "Doctor Ling has given you his seal of approval!"

"How long have I been here?" The memory of the fire came flooding back to Tom, suddenly. It brought him totally awake with a tingling shot of adrenalin.

"About a day."

"What about Anita?"

"Doctor Ling's with her. She's in intensive care."

"...and Ben?"

"Did I hear someone mention my name?" Tom heard the metallic swish of a hospital privacy curtain, and he rolled over to see his friend lying in a bed next to his. The young Indian smiled at Tom mischievously.

"Except for those fancy pink hands, you look okay, buddy!"

Tom remembered his burns. He held up his hands and looked at them. They had indeed been sprayed with *Medi-cote*, an antibiotic which left a protective film, like new skin, over a wound. It kept the dirt out, but let air in for healing. It would wear off gradually. Tom had once asked a doctor why *Medi-cote* was pink. The man looked at him as though he had missed the obvious.

"Why, so we know it's *there*, of course!"

But why *pink*?

"How long do I have to stay here?" Tom asked his father.

"You can leave any time you want, but I'd put some clothes on, first, if I were you."

Tom blushed and looked at the hospital gowns he and Ben were wearing.

The elder Swift smiled. "You'll find some things

hanging in the closet. After you get dressed, meet me outside. The Captain wants to see us."

"Has he been down to the lab?" Tom asked. The young man got out of his bed gingerly. Every muscle in his body protested the act.

"That's between you and him. It's not what he wants to talk to *us* about."

"Dad..."

Tom Swift, Senior turned from the infirmary hatch and looked at his son. "I know," he said, gently. "It was an accident. You did the best you could. I'm just glad you're all right." Then, he ducked slightly, to clear the top of the hatch, and left the infirmary.

Tom's father was waiting for him at the ship's main lift. "Bridge," he said into the control speaker.

"Thank you," said a machine voice. There was a sensation of movement. The lift was controlled by the ship's computer and the voice activation worked on the same principle as the EXCOM circuit in Tom's robot. The "thank you" response was just a matter of simple programming. The AUDIGEN—AUDIO GENerator—circuit manufactured the voice. Tom's robot would have AUDIGEN, too, but the system would be much more refined to enable the robot to converse with humans.

If there still *was* a robot.

"Any news from the Argus Probe?" Tom asked.

"No, we're getting the usual crazy signals from it. The thing's been no good at all since it landed on Io. The radiation must have got to it."

27

Io was the innermost of the "Galilean" moons of Jupiter. The scientist and astronomer, Galileo had discovered Io and her three sister moons, Callisto, Europa and Ganymede in 1610, and had named them after characters in the myths about Zeus, the king of the Olympian gods, also called Jupiter. They were Jupiter's largest moons and the ones of prime interest to scientists.

The Argus Probe had been named, by Tom, after a character with a hundred eyes, in the myth of Io. To Tom, the name had seemed appropriate for the probe, designed and built by Swift Enterprises. Its "hundred eyes" would scan the Galilean moons, take detailed photographs of Callisto, Ganymede, and Europa, and then land on Io. There, it would monitor the mysterious magnetic effect known as the "flux tube".

The Argus Probe had functioned perfectly throughout the first part of its mission, but after landing on Io, its signals had suddenly become so distorted that no one could make any sense out of the data.

"Bridge," the computer announced, flatly. The doors of the lift slid open and Tom and his father walked out into the brain centre of the *Daniel Boone*. A short distance away, the Captain, in a U.S. Navy jumper, stood waiting for them, leaning casually on a bulkhead support.

"Rafe," the elder Swift said. He smiled with a genuine warmth that he let few people see and held out his hand. "How's it going?"

The two men shook hands. The Captain was a full ten centimetres shorter than either Tom or his father, but beefier in build. The beef was all muscle.

"Captain Barrot," Tom said, more formally. As far as he knew, his father was the only man on board ever permitted to call the Captain by his first name. That stemmed partially from his unique relationship with the Swifts, and partially from his attitude about the Navy.

Until the *Daniel Boone* project, Rafe Barrot had been one of the Swift Enterprises' senior grade freighter pilots—the youngest in the company's history. During the construction of the ship, the daring young pilot was drafted to help ferry supplies and materials to the work site from Earth and from the *New America* space colony.

Swift Enterprises was the chief contractor on the *Daniel Boone*, but it was a government project, and all during the construction phase, there had been quite a bit of controversy over how the giant ship would be outfitted and crewed. All of the branches of the military service wanted the contract and the bidding was lively. That's where Rafe Barrot had figured prominently.

"The Navy needs you, son," had been the words of Admiral Harris. Rafe Barrot loved to tell this story and he did a fair imitation of the crusty Admiral's voice. "For forty years, I've had to sit and watch those Air Force boys get all the glory for the space programme while the Navy got the 'privilege' of fishing for the capsules.

"No more! The Navy's got to grow or die and I say the Navy should be up there! Space is the ocean of the universe and that's Navy territory!" No one had taken the old Admiral too seriously, until it was disclosed that of all the armed services who'd put in bids for the *Daniel Boone*, the Navy had put in the lowest, and had won.

Now the question was, who would Captain the ship? The *Daniel Boone* was the first exploratory ship of its kind and there were no regulation manuals on how to command such a ship.

The answer was in Rafe Barrot's background in the Naval Air Force and in his experience as a space pilot on large vessels. So Barrot had been called back into service. He'd been "drafted"—with his permission, of course—and restored to the rank of Captain.

The years as a civilian had left their imprint on him, however. Tom was acutely aware of how sharply Barrot's relaxed manner contrasted with his crew of starched career Navy men. It did not mean that the Captain took his job any less seriously than they did, it was just his way. Together, he and the crew were writing that Navy regulations manual for star ships.

Rafe Barrot smiled his usual lazy smile and motioned for the two Swifts to follow him. "We've decided on a location for *Ganymede Base*," he said. "Come to the chartroom with me. I'd like to hear your feedback."

Tom recognized that this was a courtesy being extended to him and his father by Barrot. It came out of their long-standing friendship, rather than duty. Even though Swift Enterprises had built the *Daniel Boone*, he and his father were civilians, and part of the scientific staff of the expedition. They had no say at all in matters pertaining to the running of the ship. In fact, few civilians were ever permitted on the bridge and few of the Navy crew were ever seen in sections of the ship assigned to the scientists and other civilian personnel.

The chartroom of the *Daniel Boone* bore little

resemblance to a traditional, ocean-going ship's chartroom, where the captain of the vessel went to plot a course. There were no charts here, only a computer terminal and a giant wall screen.

Barrot sat down at the terminal and punched out a code. The wall screen was suddenly filled with the harsh terrain of Ganymede, the third moon out from Jupiter's surface and the largest of the planet's major moons.

"What you're looking at, is a series of satellite photos taken by Argus," explained Rafe. "They were linked together by our computer to form a continuity map that we could work from. The longitude and latitude lines are the computer's, too."

"What a mess," said Tom, as he looked at the abrupt surface contrasts of the moon. Barrot and his father laughingly agreed.

"That's a perfect description," said the elder Swift.

When seen this way, the irregularities in the features of the moon stood out in sharp contrast from one another. Craters, ringed with wide, bright haloes of ice, lay next to broad smooth plains. Next to that, regions of craggy mountains could be seen. Throughout everything, a network of grooves and ridges, called *sulci*, branched and intersected, cutting into the surface. They testified to Ganymede's history of violent surface activity that resembled Earth's own. Tom's overall impression of the moon was of a puzzle world, put together of left-over bits and pieces of other planets. To top it all off, a blanket of ice, hundreds of kilometres thick, covered the entire surface.

In its way, Ganymede was no more inhospitable than Europa or Callisto, as a choice of a base for operations. Io, a volcanic world, was, of course, out of the running. Ganymede had been chosen as a compromise. It was close enough to study Jupiter and the other moons, but far enough away from the surface of the highly radioactive planet to permit adequate long-term effective shielding. Its gravity was also very close to that of the Earth's moon, although the period of rotation was much shorter for Ganymede because of the proximity of massive Jupiter.

Rafe Barrot punched another code and the general view was replaced by the specific region of craters, which resembled the Earth's moon. Barrot worked the console again, and a large crater jumped into view.

"We've chosen a site next to the largest crater in the area, Galgamesh. That way, we'll have more than enough space to land equipment and conduct experiments. We're looking at approximately sixty-five degrees West, latitude, a hundred and thirty-seven degrees South, longitude.

"We'll be going into Ganymede orbit in about three weeks from today," he finished.

"I'll make the announcement," Tom Swift, Senior, said, quietly.

This is it, Tom thought. A shiver of excitement went through him. Part of him did not want to get to Ganymede. Not yet, anyway. The "getting there" had been too much fun. Now, he was three weeks from setting his foot down on the icy crust of another world.

CHAPTER FOUR

Tom Swift, Junior, opened the door of Anita's room in the Intensive Care ward of the ship's infirmary. "Anita," he called out softly. There was no answer.

"Maybe she's asleep," whispered Ben, next to him.

Tom opened the door a bit wider and poked his head inside the room. "Anita?"

"Well?" whispered Ben, anxiously.

There was a sound of glass breaking against the door. Tom withdrew his head quickly.

"You could have taken the flowers out, first, Anita," he called out. "I had quite a time getting the hydroponics people to give them to me!"

The hydroponics section of the *Daniel Boone* was mainly responsible for putting fresh oxygen into the ship's air circulation system by growing a variety of plants in huge tanks of water and nutrients.

The technique of "water gardening", itself, was ancient. The Aztecs had used it to "farm" Lake Tenochtitlan, in the great central valley of what was now, Mexico. They had had very little land upon which to grow crops so they had woven huge mats of reeds and bullrushes. Then they had dredged up the rich soil of the lake bottom and spread it on the mats. Flowers, crops, and even trees grew on these *chinampas*, their roots growing through the floor of the rafts and down into the water.

In modern times, it was discovered that plants placed in a chamber with a high level of carbon dioxide will gradually absorb it and give off oxygen as a by-product, when sunlight is present.

The hydroponics section of the ship was an integral part of its operation. But there were other advantages. The fresh vegetables grown on the ship relieved the monotony of the freeze-dried food, and the occasional fresh flowers relieved the visual monotony. The flowers, however, were a rarity, and highly prized.

There was silence from inside Anita's room. Tom stuck his head inside the door again. The redhead was sitting up in her bed and Tom could see that she was mad.

"Get out," she yelled at him. "I told them I didn't want anyone to see me like this!"

"It's all right, Anita..."

Tom withdrew his head from the room abruptly, and Ben heard the sound of a solid object crash against the door.

"You and your old robot!" the boys heard from inside the room. "I hope you all spring a leak in your space suits and choke!"

This time, Ben put his head in the room.

"You don't mean that, Anita…" A flying hairbrush narrowly missed his eye.

"I think she does," said Tom, as Ben jumped back. The two boys stood in front of the door, feeling helpless.

"In a way, I can understand how she feels," said Tom. "She's on the greatest expedition in the history of mankind and she's confined to a bed. I'd be pretty crazy, if it were me."

"I wish she'd let me look at her leg," said Ben. "Doctor Ling said that it was totally dead, but he's no computer expert. Other than that, she's all right. If I could just get a look at it, I might be able to help her walk again."

Just then, the doors of the lift opened and Tom Swift, Senior, walked toward them.

"How's Anita?" he asked.

"She can't walk and she's pretty upset. That's it in a nutshell, Dad," said Tom.

"Let me talk to her," said the elder Swift, opening the door as he spoke.

"Dad, I wouldn't…"

The boys heard a crash of glass against the door and then they heard Anita gasp. They followed Tom, Senior into the room.

"Oh, Mister Swift," cried Anita, "I'm so sorry! I thought…never mind what I thought!"

"I haven't been greeted that way since I was Tom's age," Swift chuckled. The boys noticed that the man was casually brushing water off his jumper.

"I'm so sorry," continued Anita, "I just let my emotions get away with me sometimes. This trip has been so exciting, and now, just before we're about to land on Ganymede, this happens. I'm going to miss the rest of the trip!" The young girl burst into tears.

"Nonsense," said Tom, Senior. "Some of the finest minds in the scientific community are on board this ship, not to mention two rather integral members of the Swift family! Do you think, for one minute, that we'd let a choice scientific opportunity like this one pass? You will *not* spend the rest of this trip in bed, young lady!"

Anita sniffed and blew her nose. Then she laughed self-consciously. "N-no, I guess I was being foolish."

"That's better," said the elder Swift. Tom and Ben winked at Anita.

"Do you feel up to a trip to the lab?" Tom asked Anita. "We haven't been down there since the accident."

"If you're sure I won't be in the way," the young woman replied, but she was already getting out of her bed. Tom moved to help the girl with a pair of crutches which were leaning against a table next to her bed.

"Just give me ten minutes to get dressed," she said, excitedly.

Tom looked at the lab door in silence. He was almost afraid to open it, but he knew his father, Ben and Anita were waiting for him. He reached inside the steel panel recessed into the bulkhead and pushed the red handle up. Instantly, he heard a hissing sound, as air was pumped back into the lab. A minute later, a buzzer sounded. That was the "all clear" signal. The lab had been filled with air and the pressure equalized. Tom turned the wheel, unlocking the chamber, and went in.

A layer of thick soot covered everything. It was sticky to the touch. That testified to melted plastic insulation that had become airborne during the fire.

The robot stood where it had been left. It, too, was covered with the sticky soot. Tom's heart fell as he saw that the only thing left of the arm were the steel struts. Metal globules from the bulkhead were melted onto it. The fire had been very hot.

"I guess it's back to square one," said Ben, dejectedly.

"Don't be too sure," said Tom. "I built this robot for outer space. In a way, this was a good test for it, because if it can't survive a fire in a laboratory, it's got no chance on a place like Io. The arm was unshielded and we'll definitely have to rebuild that, but the rest of it should be all right."

Tom brushed the thick soot off the light on the sensorframe. "There's power inside," he announced.

"Congratulations, son," said his father. "You've still got a lot of work ahead of you if you want to get the robot done before we have to start setting up Ganymede base."

"That's right," said Tom. He looked around at the destroyed lab. How would they ever get the lab back into condition so they could work? Most of the equipment and all of Tom's tools had been destroyed. When the *Daniel Boone* went into orbit around Ganymede, and they began building the base, his father would need him *and* the robot.

"You'll need a place to work," said the elder

Swift. "It won't be worth your time to restore this lab. Come with me." The young people followed Tom, Senior into the lift. They went up two decks and down a long corridor.

"This is your private quarters, Dad," said Tom, aghast.

"No, that's my private quarters," his father replied, pointing two hatches down from the one he was opening with a magnetic key. "This is my private *lab*."

Tom and Ben helped Anita through the hatch. Then the three young people followed Tom Swift, Senior, inside the laboratory. Their mouths fell open in astonishment.

The blackness of space surrounded and enveloped them. Where the walls should have been, great crystal clear panels of the strongest polyglass known to man had been set into the very framework of the ship.

"Jewels on black velvet," said Tom. He was mesmerised by the millions of pinpoints of light that dotted the blackness.

"We've really gone to the stars," Anita muttered. "We've been so busy since this trip started, that I haven't even had the chance to go up to the observation deck and look out. The inside of this ship has been my whole world. I forgot what it was like outside!"

"As many times as I've worked in here since the expedition started, I never get tired of just looking out there," said the elder Swift. "In a few minutes, you'll get a real sight. We should be coming up on Jupiter."

"When you're inside the ship, you can't tell we're spinning," said Ben. The *Daniel Boone*, shaped like a giant cylinder, rotated on its axis once every 114 seconds. That gave its passengers a close approximation of Earth-normal gravity on the perimeter.

"It's funny how we humans use the Earth to measure our lives," said Tom. "A day, for example, is twenty-four hours. But that's only because it takes our planet that long to make one complete revolution on its axis. On Ganymede, the days will be a hundred and sixty-eight hours long because it shows the same face to Jupiter all the time and therefore its period of rotation is equal to its revolution."

"Or how about a *year*," said Anita, frowning. "It takes Jupiter twelve Earth years to make one complete revolution around the sun. A girl could age a lot in a year like that!" She was still frowning when she finished, but then she broke into laughter. Tom, his father, and Ben laughed with her.

The hypnotic effect of the view from the lab was broken by Anita's joke and the three young people began to look around with a new amazement.

Every piece of testing equipment imaginable had been fitted into the room.

"Great Scott," exclaimed Tom, "we'd have to go all over the ship to find some of this stuff!"

"Help Anita up onto the examining table, son," said Tom, Senior. The young inventor put Anita's crutches aside and lifted her up onto a big segmented table near the centre of the lab floor. The table was motorised and any part of it could be moved so that the table was in exactly the right spot for any experiment.

The elder Swift motioned to Ben and the computer tech trotted over to where the older man was pulling a large machine on wheels out of a bank of other equipment. Together, they wheeled it over to where Tom and Anita were waiting.

"What's that?" Anita asked. The big machine had rows of dials and gauges, an alpha-numeric key board, and a blank screen that looked like a computer monitor.

"It's a general electronics testing peripheral," said Tom. "The power source is the ship's computer, but the peripheral has its own programs for testing. It just increases the versatility of our computer without a lot of new programming, that nobody else would have a use for."

"I've never seen one quite like it," said Ben. "Normally, it would take several pieces of equipment to get a really accurate reading on anything."

"We planned for limited space on the *Daniel Boone*," said Tom's father. "This was one of the ways we did it. If I think the machine is useful enough, Swift Enterprises will put it into production when we get back to Earth."

"I guess that's how a lot of inventions come into being," mused Anita. "You have a problem that must be solved and when the old ways don't work, you have to think up something new."

"Sometimes people find other uses for the invention, too," volunteered Ben.

"And those other uses spark new inventions," finished Tom. "Off hand, I can't think of any invention that wasn't the product of several other ideas put together in a new way. That's the inventing biz and that's progress, too. It's one big cycle." Tom and his father, and Ben finished hooking the machine up to the ship's computer terminal in the lab, and then Tom connected the tester's leads to Anita's wrist controller. Ben pulled up a lab stool and sat down in front of the tester's keyboard. He looked at Tom, expectantly.

"We think that your computer's internal power source is dead because you can't move your leg," said Tom. "Let's see if we can get a voltage pattern, just to make sure." Ben worked over the keyboard for a moment. An oscilloscope grid appeared on the screen. A spot of light appeared at the zero line on the scope and stretched across the grid, flat.

"No pattern," said Ben. "The power source was probably burned out by the high voltage surge that occurred when you yanked the adaptor lead out of the robot."

"I agree," said Tom. "Delicate transistors, and especially diodes, don't like voltage surges."

"That's what you were trying to warn me about," Anita said sheepishly.

"I should have phrased my warning better," said Tom. He patted Anita on the shoulder.

"Put power to the central processing unit," said Tom's father. "Let's see if there's any continuity."

"Putting current to the CPU," said Ben. "Nothing's coming out."

"Even the motherboard is junk," sighed the redhead, referring to her computer's main circuit board. "That's the ball game."

"No, it's not," said Tom, firmly. "Ben and I put the *Davy Cricket* together out of almost nothing after my original racer blew up! Our computer was sabotaged *twice* and we still made it into the race!"

"And you won, too! Don't forget *that*," said An-

41

ita, dryly. She had met Tom and Ben while building her own racer back on the *New America* space colony. The three young people had been contestants in the annual Three-Corner Race which had been run from *New America*, to the *Sunflower* space colony, from there to the Armstrong Moon base, and back to *New America*. The *Davy Cricket* had started late, but because of Tom's fusion drive, he and Ben had won. Anita's racer, the *Valkyrie* had come in second.

"We can at least get you walking," said Ben.

"We can do more than that," chuckled Tom's father. Tom, Ben and Anita looked at the elder Swift with puzzlement as he unlocked a sturdy metal closet and took out a black plastic box that fit in the palm of his hand. "Do you remember the microcomputer chip design we discussed over dinner several months ago, Tom?"

"Of course," said Tom, excitedly. "I've been so busy with the robot that I forgot about it!"

Tom, Senior saw that Ben and Anita had puzzled expressions on their faces. He smiled at them apologetically. "Tom and I came up with the design for the chip after a minor accident that had taken place that afternoon in the nuclear research lab.

"The techs were conducting final experiments on the decontamination solution that we're going to be using on this expedition to combat Jupiter's radiation. They were behind safety shielding and they were using waldos to mix the solution in the experimental chamber..."

"Waldos are those robot arms they use to do things when it's not safe for humans to be close up, aren't they?" Anita asked.

"That's right," said Tom's father. "The techs were having trouble with the experiment because the waldos weren't sensitive enough. It took them longer than it should have to complete the experiment and they almost dropped one of the vials of solution.

"That night, Tom and I decided we needed a more sensitive chip to control the movement of the waldos so we designed it right there at the dinner table!"

"That was also the night Mom got upset because we let the roast beef get cold while we talked about micro chips," chuckled Tom, fondly. He swallowed hard to control the pang of homesickness he felt every time he thought of his mother, back in New Mexico, waiting for her husband and her son who were quite literally a million kilometres away. Tom could tell that his father's thoughts were there, too.

The elder Swift opened the black plastic box and held it out for the three young people to see. Inside, lay a centimetre square of epoxy and metal. Some tiny wires protruded from one edge of it.

"I don't see anything inside the *package*," exclaimed Ben, using the technical name for the tiny epoxy square.

Tom, Senior motioned for Tom, Ben and Anita to follow him. He walked over to a work bench with a huge microscope on it. Then he opened the instrument drawer and selected a pair of forceps. He slowly and carefully took the epoxy square out of the box and placed it under the microscope. "Take a look," he said.

"You go first, Ben," Tom said to his friend. It

43

was obvious that the young Indian computer tech was very excited by the new microcomputer chip. He had an almost supernatural ability with computers and, in Tom's opinion, Benjamin Franklin Walking Eagle was the foremost expert on the state of the art in computer hardware.

Ben peered through the microscope at the chip. He was silent the whole time and when he stood up, there was a look of pure rapture on his face. "Now *that's* what I call beautiful," he said, then his face broke into a wide grin. He stepped aside to let Tom and Anita have a look.

"It needs to be tested in a working situation," said the elder Swift. He looked directly at Anita. "I'd like *you* to put it to the test, Ms Thorwald."

Anita looked embarrassed for a moment, then she smiled, shyly. "I can't refuse an offer like that, Mister Swift, but Tom needs to put the time in on his robot. He'll be running all over the ship between the two projects. He might not get the robot finished before we get to Ganymede."

Tom, Senior, turned to his son. "Move the robot up here. I'm not going to have much time to work in this lab from now on. I need to help Rafe Barrot plan the set-up of Ganymede Base."

"That's how we got into trouble in the first place," said Tom. "There's something wrong with the robot and we don't know what it is. The accident in the lab happened when we tried to move it down to engineering."

"Ah, the burden of the inventor," said the elder Swift, sympathetically. "I've had to discover many of my mistakes the hard way, too. There's a simple solution, though. We can borrow a chain hoist and a cart from the people down in cargo. Then you can wheel the robot up here. I may not be captain of the good ship *Daniel Boone*, but I have *that* much influence!"

"Look," said Anita. The young woman pointed toward the foreward window of the lab as the brightly coloured edge of Jupiter appeared. No-one said anything for a long time.

CHAPTER FIVE

"I still don't believe it," exclaimed Ben.

Tom Swift, Junior shrugged his shoulders and smiled apologetically at his friend. "We ran the robot's complete program and did circuit checks on every part of him. Nothing showed up. The rebuilt arm checks out perfectly and the robot hasn't malfunctioned since we reactivated him. The only conclusion I can draw is that the bug that caused the accident was somewhere in the arm that got burned up."

The two young men entered the lab. Since Tom's father had given them the use of the facility, Tom, Ben and Anita had spent all of their waking moments in it. It had become a home.

Anita looked up from a microfiche viewer as Tom and Ben walked in. Next to her, the robot turned the domed centre of its sensorframe until the deep blue-violet "eyes" of its two camera lenses were directed at Tom. The robot watched the young inventor as he moved around the lab.

The robot's sensorframe had been completed only a few days. It was obvious, however, that the mechanoid already had a definite preference for its camera "sight" over sonarscan and the photo-sensitive arrays. Was it a quirk of the central processing unit? Tom was not sure. It was, however, the kind of "personality trait" he had hoped for in the robot. The element of random choice. A human quality. It made the robot more than a machine.

And today would mark the beginning of a new phase in Tom's relationship with the robot. The audigen chip had been mounted in its package and today, it would be connected to its printed circuit card, called the PC card. Communication with the robot would no longer be restricted to task-oriented commands.

"Good morning," Anita said, smiling mischievously. Tom laughed. The three young people were always amused when Earth-born expressions in the language failed. Technically, it was *morning*, because they were beginning their waking cycle. But inside the *Daniel Boone*, the terms "day" and "night" hardly applied. The sun was now so far behind them that it had become just another bright point in the blackness of space. There was no planet or moon for it to hide behind. There wouldn't be one until they went into Jupiter orbit a few cycles from now.

Jupiter orbit. It seemed so distant, yet already, the pocked and lined face of Ganymede filled the view from the lab's foreward windows. Every time they saw it, the surface details became sharper. Every sleep cycle, the planet-sized moon filled more and more of their dreams.

"How did Ben take the news about the bug?" Anita asked, teasingly.

"It was traumatic for him, but he'll pull through," answered Tom. The young inventor glanced at Ben to see if he had picked up on the joke.

Ben shook his head, obviously amused.

"It's pretty hard for *me* to accept the fact that we were almost killed by some electronic 'glitch' that we never even found," Anita said. "It *does* seem to be the only answer, though."

Tom grimaced. "The idea of being haunted by this for the rest of my life doesn't appeal to me. I'll never know what I did wrong. I hate to make mistakes, but when I do, I like to correct them and learn from the experience."

"And we have no way of knowing when or if the malfunction will raise its ugly head again," said Anita. The joking mood had left her. "Do we have a robot we can't trust?"

The three young people looked at each other in silence for a moment. It was a question that they had each asked themselves many times.

Ben shrugged his shoulders, breaking the sombre mood that had descended upon the three friends. "We used the computer to check everything out. If computers don't lie, then we have nothing to worry about. You all know how I stand on *that* subject."

"Besides," added Tom, "the whole space programme has been plagued by 'glitches' since it started. A lot of the early launches were postponed for hours and even *days* because some fifty cent valve didn't work. It's all part of the exploration game!"

"Look," Anita broke in, "could we change the subject? We never really came to any conclusions about whether the robot listens to us when we talk about him, or even if he's capable of anything approaching an emotional reaction because of what he hears. But I can't shake the uncomfortable feeling that I'm gossiping about someone in front of them!"

Tom looked at Anita, surprised at the emotion in her voice. She looked away, hurriedly.

"I-I'm sorry," she mumbled, turning her back to Tom, "I haven't been in control of myself, lately. I guess I'm just tired or something."

"I think we've all been working too hard," said Tom, gently. "You and Ben and I ought to go to the *hub* and get a little exercise."

The *Daniel Boone* was a great rotating cylinder. The rotation created an artificial gravity inside the ship so that the humans could carry on their lives as normally as possible. The hub was the centre axis of the ship and there, a weightless condition existed. For the amusement and the health of the passengers on the ship, the hub had been sectioned into athletic courts where several different kinds of null-gravity sports were played.

Anita's face brightened. "I haven't been up there since the accident! It'll give me a chance to really test out my new leg! We need another body if we're going to play null-gravity handball, though."

Tom smiled devilishly. "And I know just who to ask, too—my father!"

50

"Oh no," Anita protested. "That will give you an unfair advantage!" She knew of the elder Swift's reputation in the game even though he'd only been playing for a short time. Tom had introduced him to it on their last trip to the *New America* space colony. Tom had to admit that his father had shown an enviable natural ability to play the game well.

Anita's mood changed so abruptly that it caught Tom off guard. "You haven't seen much of your father these past few weeks, and it bothers you, doesn't it? You're very worried about him."

"I-I suppose so," said Tom, suddenly feeling very uncomfortable. It was as if the young woman had looked into the most private and secret corner of his mind. He *had* been worried about his father, who had a habit of over-working himself in critical situations. On Earth, he had his secretary, Marguerite, and his chief assistant, Gene Larson, to stop him from doing that. But they were not on the *Daniel Boone*. Frankly, Tom had to admit that he had been feeling very guilty about spending so much time working on the robot and very little time checking up on his father even though the elder Swift would never have tolerated being checked up on by his son.

"You shouldn't feel guilty," said Anita.

"How did you know what I was thinking?" asked Tom.

"I didn't," replied Anita. She looked at Tom with a puzzled expression on her face. "All of a sudden, I could just tell what you were *feeling*. The funny part of it is, I don't know how I knew. I don't know why I feel the way I do about the robot, either, I just *do*!"

51

Tom looked over at the robot and caught his breath. His eyes met the unblinking camera lenses. It *is* more than just a machine, he thought to himself. He turned to Anita and put his hand on her shoulder. "Let's finish the audigen circuit so we can find out what the robot thinks," he said.

Anita smiled up at him and then nodded in agreement.

Tom knew that the audigen circuit *he* had designed would put a big load on the robot's central processing unit. Usually, audigen was delegated to TTL circuitry—transistor-transistor logic. That way the central processing unit or "brain" of a computer or a robot could concentrate on higher level duties. That was how the audigen circuit of the *Daniel Boone*'s lift worked.

You couldn't have a conversation with the lift, however. TTL circuits couldn't handle anything that sophisticated.

Tom walked over to the work bench which Ben was hunched over and looked over his friend's shoulder. The young man had a small soldering iron with a needle-fine tip in his hand and he was peering through a large adjustable magnifying glass at a thin, rectangular wafer of metal. Through the magnifying glass, Tom could see the tiny lines, or *traces* of the electrical circuits that had been photographically etched onto the wafer. Ben touched the point of the soldering iron to the wafer near the base of the epoxy square that had been mounted in the centre of it. A thin column of smoke rose from the place the iron had touched. Ben pushed the magnifying glass down closer and peered into it for a moment. Then he sat back and looked at Tom with a satisfied expression on his face.

"The chip's mounted," he said.

"Let's get it in, then," said Tom. He picked up the small printed circuit card with a pair of forceps and walked over to where the robot stood, watching him silently.

"Unlock the control unit," said Tom to the mechanoid. There was a clicking sound and then the whir of a tiny electric motor. A drawer-like section came foreward out of the robot's chest.

There were five PC cards standing upright in the drawer and a place for a sixth card. Tom inserted the new card into the empty spot, using the forceps. He was very careful not to touch any of the other cards with his hands. The chemicals in human perspiration could do a lot of damage to electrical components. He made sure that the card was connected properly and then visually inspected the other components in the control unit. "Lock the control unit," he said to the robot, when he was satisfied. The electric motor pulled the drawer back into the robot's chest. It locked shut with a faint click.

There was a scratching sound that resembled some of the old recordings made on plastic discs that Tom's father had played for him when he was very young. Then, in an emotionless, electronic voice, the robot said, "Control unit . . . locked . . . Tom."

Tom, Ben and Anita were stunned. No one said a word for a few seconds. They just stared at the robot, who stared back at them. Finally, Tom broke the silence. There was awe in his voice.

"I designed him to talk, I built him to talk, and now I can't believe he can talk!"

Ben laughed. "The inventor is overwhelmed by his invention! Say something to it, Tom."

Tom couldn't think of anything to say. Julius Caesar, Abraham Lincoln, and Neil Armstrong had all faced the same dilemma and their words had survived through history as inspiration for mankind. Would Armstrong have delayed his first moon walk until he had thought of something to say? Probably. First words were important.

His mind was a blank. Here stood the end result of months of planning and work. All of his creative energy and time had been channelled into the robot. And now, when he should be having his moment of supreme glory and accomplishment, he couldn't think of anything to say. The silence was growing awkward. "Hello, robot," he said, finally.

"Hello…Tom," said the robot.

Behind him, Tom heard Anita start to giggle. She stopped when the robot turned to her and asked, "Anita . . . functioning . . . well?"

"He spoke to me," she gasped.

Tom felt a twinge of the apprehension that had been nagging at him since he started the robot project. It was the fear of "unleashing" something on the world that he, the inventor, had no control over. The robot had spoken without being asked a question, and Tom knew that he had invented a mechanical "being" that could think for itself far more independently than its programming limit.

Could the robot willingly do violence to a human? No. Tom had made very sure of that, at least. Still, the thought of coexisting with a robot that had an unpredictable personality was a bit scary. It would take getting used to.

"We can't go on calling it, 'robot', you know," said Ben. "It should have a name."

"I've been thinking about that," said Tom.

"What about an acronym like 'Tom's Intelligent Machine'. That's 'TIM'," suggested Anita.

"Somehow, that's not dignified enough for him," said Tom.

"You could always pick a name out of mythology," said Ben. "Call him Hercules, or something."

"That just doesn't feel right for him," said Tom, frowning in thought. "He's too intellectual for that. In fact, I've been thinking of calling him Aristotle, after my favourite Greek philosopher."

"Aristotle?" said Anita.

"What kind of name is that for a robot?" asked Ben. "I mean, it sounds okay, but I don't understand the significance."

"He lived in the third century, B.C. and he was Alexander the Great's tutor. He was also the first philosopher to realize that all knowledge comes from pre-existing knowledge. He was an historian, a doctor, and a scientist as well as a philosopher and I think that Aristotle is the perfect name for the robot!"

"Pleased to meet you, Aristotle," said Ben to the robot.

"I am greatly..." The robot paused for a few seconds, then said, "I have no word in my vocabulary bank. My components are in harmonious synchronization with the name, Aristotle."

Tom smiled. "Humans often make comparisons in terms of pleasure and pain, Aristotle. Pleasure is harmonious synchronization, pain is the opposite."

"I am...pleased," said Aristotle.

"This calls for a celeb..." Tom was cut off in mid-sentence by the loud, high-pitched wail of the ship's siren.

"What's wrong," asked Anita, fearfully.

"Nothing's wrong," said Tom, excitedly. "That's the signal! We're entering Ganymede orbit! Let's get down to the recreation room and watch!"

The three young people ran for the lab hatch. Ben and Anita ducked through first and their footsteps echoed down the corridor. Tom paused at the hatch. "Come on, Aristotle! I don't want your sensors to miss this!"

Aristotle moved foreward a few centimetres, then stopped. Tom grimaced impatiently. "What's wrong?" he asked.

"I am a faulty mechanism," replied the robot.

Tom straightened up and looked at the robot. "Explain," he said formally.

"During my construction, I malfunctioned and caused the human, Anita, to shut down. The cause of the malfunction is unknown, therefore, the probability exists that I may again go against my programming, as you stated, Tom."

So the robot *had* heard and stored everything he, Ben and Anita had said about it! What's more, the information had been interpreted on a level that Tom had not thought was possible. In other words, he now had a robot with a guilt complex! "I require that you come with me to the recreation room, Aristotle. We'll discuss your malfunction later," said Tom. He knew that the robot would not and *could not* disobey a direct command.

"Yes, Tom," said Aristotle, moving forward again, unhesitatingly, this time.

CHAPTER SIX

The *Daniel Boone*'s rec room was packed with people by the time Tom, Ben, Anita and Aristotle got there. Scientists, technicians and civilian crew were all mixed together and talking excitedly. Tom even spotted quite a few Navy uniforms in the crowd and that was very unusual.

A few people stared at Aristotle, but the attention of most of the crowd was focussed on the excitement of the moment. Besides, robots were not all that unusual a sight for the scientists and technicians of the *Daniel Boone*. There were a number of them in storage in the ship's hold. They would be an important part of the work force of *Ganymede Base*. They were not, however, as sophisticated as Aristotle.

Tom saw his father at the opposite end of the

room, near the giant wall screen normally used for computer games. The elder Swift looked in Tom's direction a few times, but Tom couldn't tell if his father had seen him. The young inventor saw his father say something to the Navy officer sitting at the rec room's computer console and suddenly, Captain Rafe Barrot's voice came over the com. The room quieted instantly.

The Captain was giving orders to the bridge crew. It must be very busy up there, Tom thought, as he listened to the sound of the *Daniel Boone*'s instruments and of the crew performing their assigned duties.

Then, quite suddenly, the wall screen sprang into life with a spectacular view of Ganymede, framed by the huge marbled surface of Jupiter. Tom had never seen anything more beautiful...or more alien.

His mind refused to accept the proportions, for one thing. It was not like looking at the Earth from the moon, as he had done while visiting Armstrong Base. Jupiter was thirteen hundred times larger, in volume, than the Earth!

Of course, Tom knew that they were looking at just the violently swirling upper atmosphere of the planet. A short distance below that gaseous layer, was a liquid hydrogen sea, and below that, it was believed, lay a small rocky core about the size of the Earth.

A cheer went up from the people in the room as four tiny orbiting specks suddenly came into view at Ganymede's equator. The equipment pods sent from Earth months ago. All of them had survived the rigours of space and the hazards of attaining Ganymede orbit. They would need all of the equipment in the pods when they began construction of *Ganymede Base*.

Abruptly, Tom felt a small change in the ship's rhythm. It was subtle and he was surprised that he had noticed it at all.

The *Daniel Boone* was a fusion drive ship. There was no engine—and thus no engine sounds—in the conventional sense. The heart of the system was made up of five clusters of ten laser beams in what was called a "target chamber". They were set up so that the beams converged at a central point. About once each second, a microscopic fuel pellet, made up of deuterium and tritium—the heavy isotopes of hydrogen—was injected ballistically into the target chamber. The laser system actually tracked the pellet to the centre of the combustion chamber and then blew it up. The amount of energy released was staggering.

The rhythm changed again. Tom looked at Ben and Anita. They had noticed it, too.

"The sequence of deceleration manoeuvres for geosynchronous orbit has begun, Tom," said Aristotle.

Tom looked at Aristotle in wonderment. Was it possible for a robot to be excited? He was probably just imagining things. It had been a long trip.

In reality, the *Daniel Boone* had been in deceleration for several weeks now, but *geosynchronous* orbit meant that the ship would decelerate to match the exact orbital speed of Ganymede as the moon travelled around Jupiter.

Like the Earth's moon, the Galilean satellites presented the same face toward Jupiter. They did not rotate. That was an important factor in the placement of the instruments the scientists would use to study Jupiter and her moons. It was *very* important to the location of *Ganymede Base* because of the tremendous radiation given off by Jupiter. The base would be located near the south pole of Ganymede, on the dark side. The *Daniel Boone*, in geosynchronous orbit with the dark side, would use the moon as a shield. The ship would never be out of communication with the base. It was all very neat and well thought-out. At least *some* of it was. Tom knew that nature and the universe had a way of gumming up even the most careful plans, sometimes.

The hub was almost deserted. Tom, his father, Ben and Anita had no trouble finding an open handball court.

"Everyone's enjoying their last few hours of full gravity, probably," Ben remarked.

"That suits me just fine," said Anita. She pushed off from the wall near the entry hatch and turned three graceful somersaults in mid-air. She finished with a half-twist and floated over to join Ben on the far side of the court. They would be a team.

"Beautifully done," exclaimed Tom.

"Your new leg appears to be functioning well," said the elder Swift.

"It's much more responsive than the old one," Anita said. "I tried a few ballet steps the other night and I was able to do some things I haven't done in a long time."

"Enough talk," said Tom, teasingly. "Let's have a game of handball!" The young inventor floated into position next to his father.

Null gravity handball had a slightly different set of rules from handball on Earth. For one thing, all surfaces of the globe-shaped court were played.

There were, of course, penalty areas for each team just to make the game interesting. The playing and penalty areas were colour-coded and marked off by black boundary lines which were off limits. Sensor mats were located under these so that judgement calls were necessary. The ball had to rebound off the opposite hemisphere from which it originated before a hit could be scored.

"Ready," said Tom to the wall speaker. A circular hatch opened and a black ball came shooting out. The gaming computer controlled the direction of the ball, but the choice was random. This time, the ball shot toward Anita's and Ben's side of the court and bounced off the wall.

"It's mine," said the elder Swift, and he launched himself into the air gracefully. He met the ball and sent it hurling toward Ben. The equal and opposite reaction of the movement sent him backward. He turned the force into a perfect backflip and landed back on his side of the court.

Ben watched the ball bounce and then he sent it back to Tom and his father.

"Mine," said Tom, and he leaped into the air to meet the ball—and knew he was going to miss it. It had been too long since he had played the game and he was rusty. He had misjudged the speed of the ball and had overshot the point where he should have contacted it. The ball went sailing by him and he sailed awkwardly into a penalty area.

Tom felt foolish as he floated back into position for the next round. His father smiled at him, sympathetically. Null-gravity handball was something you had to practice in order to stay in shape. Tom glanced at Anita and was startled to see that she

63

was looking at him. She had an intense expression on her face that Tom had never seen before. It made him very uneasy.

The computer put the ball into play again and this time, it shot within striking range of Tom Swift, Senior. He sent it over to Ben and Anita by "express". This ball stayed in play for quite a few minutes before Ben missed a shot, giving Tom and his father a point.

Tom still felt uncomfortable knowing that Anita was watching him. It made him a little angry, too. It seemed as though she was concentrating her game on him.

The weak link. He would show her that she couldn't get to him!

The computer picked Ben and Anita again. Anita watched it bounce off the court wall and then she leaped up and met it expertly. She sent it straight to Tom.

The young inventor dived to get out of the way of the projectile pushing against the nearest wall. The reaction sent him backward, out of control. He struck the court head first and pain shot through his head. At that moment, he heard Anita cry out in pain, as well. He forgot about his head and looked at her in surprise.

Tom's father and Ben were already holding on to Anita when Tom reached her. She seemed to be in pain, but Tom had not seen her get hurt.

"What happened?" he asked, anxiously. "How did she hurt herself?"

"She didn't," said Ben. "I don't understand what happened myself! I saw you hit the wall and then I heard her yell."

"I-I was watching you," said Anita, "and I knew

you were going to miss the point—I knew that *you* knew you would, too. When you hit the wall, I got a sharp pain in my head! Can someone please tell me what's happening to me? I can't control my own mind anymore!"

"There have been other incidents like this one?" Tom's father asked, alarmed.

Tom filled him in briefly on Anita's strange experiences since the accident. The elder Swift frowned thoughtfully as he listened to his son.

"Let's get down to the lab. I have a theory, but I want to run some tests before I say what I think the problem is."

Tom and Ben helped Anita onto the lab examining table while Tom, Senior got the computer test peripheral they had used to examine Anita the first time. No one spoke as he finished connecting it to the test connectors on the new leg. In the background, Aristotle watched the humans.

Tom, Senior began punching up a series of electrical tests on the console. He looked at the data on the CRT—the cathode ray tube computer screen—and frowned.

It was the kind of frown Tom knew that scientists got when they found something that they had hoped they wouldn't find, even though it meant that they were right. Tom had frowned that way many times.

"Anita is getting electrical feedback through the central processing unit in her artificial leg. It's having an unusual effect on her nervous system," said Tom's father.

"It's the new chip," said Tom.

"Anita has malfunctioned?" asked Aristotle.

The elder Swift looked at the robot and then he looked questioningly at Tom.

"Human's don't malfunction, Aristotle," said Tom. "They get sick, or hurt, or angry, happy or sad, but they don't malfunction."

"My circuits exchanged current with Anita. A malfunction occurred in her circuits at that time. Please explain, Tom."

Tom heard his father whistle softly between his teeth. "Congratulations," the elder Swift whispered to his son, "Aristotle is an amazing scientific achievement!"

Tom looked at the robot in silence for a few seconds. This was going to be difficult.

"Humans don't malfunction, Aristotle," said Tom. "Anita is a special human. She's..."

"I'm part robot, Aristotle," interrupted Anita.

Tom looked at the young woman, unsure of what to say. Her remark had caught him totally off guard.

"It *is* the best way to explain it to the robot, Tom," Anita said. "I had an accident when I was younger and the doctors had to amputate the lower part of my right leg. A computer brain 'translates' signals from my brain to the working parts of the artificial leg so that I can walk."

"I caused this part of you to malfunction," said Aristotle. "You are having difficulty which I caused. I was not programmed to cause discomfort to humans. I am an imperfect mechanism."

"*Aristotle*," yelled Tom, alarmed. "Stop that! It's not true."

"It is a fact," said the robot, stubbornly. "Truth is that which conforms with fact and reality. You are in error, Tom."

"You've been out-argued by your own pro-gramming," chortled Ben. "This is the kind of thing we computer people *love!*"

"You're not helping, Ben," said Tom. The young inventor turned to his father. "Don't just sit there, help me!"

"Who am I to interfere between the creator and his creation?" said the elder Swift, smiling mis-chievously.

"Thanks a lot!" said Tom. "Aristotle, some-times, the truth can be seen in different ways..."

"Then it is not truth, it is opinion," said the robot. "I am programmed to know the difference between truth and opinion."

"You're wrong, Aristotle!"

"That is possible. I am a faulty mechanism."

Tom's mouth fell open with astonishment. He'd been trapped. He looked at Ben but the computer tech was laughing so hard that tears were running down his cheeks. Anita and his father were trying not to laugh, but Tom could see they were losing control, too. He sat down and stared at the robot, not knowing what to say. You've won this round, chum, he thought.

Aristotle looked back at Tom, silent and un-moving, but somehow, Tom was sure the robot was laughing, too.

CHAPTER SEVEN

Tom, Ben and Anita felt the thud of the *Daniel Boone*'s lander on the surface of Ganymede through the thick layers of insulation and radiation shielding in their suits. Another work cycle had begun.

"Where's the romance of space?" Tom heard Ben groan into his suit radio.

Tom undid his safety harness and stood up stiffly. He just hadn't got enough sleep after yesterday's work cycle at the base or the one before that. Where *was* the romance of space, indeed! It did no good to complain, however. Everyone in the expedition had been pressed into hard labour. The domes had to be erected as soon as possible so that the scientists could start living at the base instead of commuting back and forth from the ship. Fortunately, the main dome would be formed today. That was some accomplishment considering the expedition's state of fatigue.

Tom looked over at Aristotle. "Let's go," he said, and watched, as the robot unfastened his own safety harness. Tom was still amazed at how nimble Aristotle's mechanical fingers were.

The young inventor motioned to Ben and Anita, and then drifted out of the hatch of the lander in the slow, graceful, "time-honoured" galloping stride that had been made famous by the first astronauts on the Earth's moon. The waltz in one-sixth G. That was the gravity of the moon, and of Ganymede. The only difference was that the surface of the moon was fine dust. On Ganymede, everyone had cleated boots that gripped the dirty ice surface. Even Aristotle had cleats on his traction pads, although the robot's tremendous weight helped to stabilise it, too.

Tom turned to make sure that Ben, Anita and Aristotle were following him, then he lumbered toward the cluster of lights that illuminated the partially constructed base camp. No one said anything. They were too tired even for conversation over their suit radios—at least the humans were.

Tom Swift looked upward. Since Ganymede had no atmosphere, the sky was not blue even though it was officially "noon", Ganymede standard time. The stars in the blackness of space did not even twinkle on this airless world. And there was a new object up there. The spaceship *Daniel Boone*. Tom sighed wistfully. It was going to be a long work cycle.

A suited, thick-set figure waved at Tom, from the base camp perimeter. The suits, with their three-centimetre-thick powdered lead shielding

70

made everyone look a little heavy, but Tom recognised the person in the suit from her body language. It was Dr. Fiona Friedman, a member of the astronomy team. They were along to study the great red spot of Jupiter. Dr. Friedman was holding up three fingers so Tom switched his suit radio to channel three, the personal communications channel.

"Your father's looking for you, Tom," said the scientist. Tom could tell she was worried about something. "He needs your help. Equipment pod number four won't come down and it's got a vital instrument package aboard and some building materials that the dome crew needs *now*. You and the robot had better 'hot foot' it over to the main dome site."

"Thanks, Doctor Friedman," said Tom. Then he laughed. "I'll run right over there." Dr. Friedman laughed and made an "okay" sign with her thickly gloved fingers.

Tom turned to his friends but Ben motioned for him to go on.

"We heard the whole thing," said the computer tech. "Anita and I have to report to our work teams right now, so we'll catch you later. We can all sit around and suck nutrient together!"

Tom shrugged his shoulders to let Ben know that he wasn't thrilled about lunching in the suits either. Going back up to the ship would take too long, however, so they didn't have much choice. He watched as Ben and Anita veered off in another direction.

The suits masked facial expressions, so exaggerated body language had become an important part of communication. Tom was always amazed at how important it was even with the suit radios. It put back the feeling and emotion into simple conversations that the radios seemed to take out.

Tom motioned for Aristotle to follow him. Together, they entered the lighted work area.

The dome work crew was inflating the "balloon", the huge plastic sack that would act as a foundation when the actual dome material was sprayed on. The floor of the structure had been finished yesterday. They had first levelled the ice, then they'd removed it in big square blocks. After that, freezer coils had been laid, then the ice blocks replaced. Heat sensors from the ice would trigger the freezer coils to come on when the ice that formed the foundation of the dome was in danger of melting. That was one problem with trying to dig a home out of the ice. Human body heat and activity tended to melt it.

When the balloon was inflated, the dome crew would begin spraying a plastic foam over it. After the foam hardened, the balloon would be removed, and support structures would be put up on the inside for safety. After that came the airlock, and after that, the whole thing had to be decontaminated and "scrubbed" of radiation. It would be a lot of work to survive on this alien world. Tom knew he'd been spoiled by the relatively effortless survival of mankind on the Earth.

A surface rover pulled up next to him, and Tom saw his father. The elder Swift held up one finger. That was the *very* private channel. The situation must be pretty serious, Tom thought.

"I'll drive you and the robot to the site where we've been bringing the pods down, Tom," said his father. "Number four isn't responding. Maybe the robot can get it down."

"What's in the pod?" asked Tom.

"Only most of the astronomy team's long range observation equipment," said his father, worriedly. "The building materials for their dome are part of that equipment package, too."

"Have you analysed the cause of this difficulty?" asked Aristotle. Tom realized with a start, that it was the first time Aristotle had spoken in hours.

"Yes," said Tom, Senior. "We think that something's gone wrong with the pod's receiver. Too much receiver resistence could cause the transmitted ground signal to be too weak. We need you to boost it, Aristotle."

"I shall do what I can," was the robot's only comment. They rode the rest of the way in silence, a silence that worried Tom. On the ship, Tom had seen Aristotle grow more and more talkative as his vocabulary increased. The machine mind was fascinating and Aristotle's learning capacity was astounding. But since the landing on Ganymede, the robot had talked less and less. It had got to the point where he only responded to direct questions.

Mechanically, he was functioning perfectly and he was an important member of the work crew. The space suits were clumsy and the humans found it difficult to do tasks that required any nimbleness. Aristotle came in very handy for those jobs, because he was not limited by a suit.

But why had he been so quiet, lately?

Presently, a group of suited figures came into view. They were clustered around a large portable transmitter. The antenna was fully extended. They waved as the Swifts' rover approached.

Tom recognised Dr. Harold Friedman among the group. The Friedmans, husband and wife, had virtually left their whole lives behind to join the Jupiter expedition. Their two sons, Ian and John, both astronomers, like their parents, made up the rest of the astronomy team. They had sold all of their property and possessions to help finance the expedition and while Harold and Fiona both had university positions waiting for them upon their return to Earth, if they wanted them, the Friedmans' future was really on the line. The equipment on pod number four could literally make or break them.

"We want you to bring the pod down as close to here as possible, Aristotle," said Tom. "Doctor Friedman will give you the code."

The rotund astronomer punched out the code signal on the transmitter. Aristotle "listened" without comment. "I am ready, Tom," the robot said, when Friedman had finished.

"Transmit the signal, Aristotle," said Tom.

"Transmitting," said the robot. "The signal has been received, Tom. The pod's landing sequence has begun."

There was a cheer from the astronomers followed by a lot of hand-shaking. Aristotle got a pat on the mainframe, too, as the group waited for the pod to come down.

"Good work," said Tom to the robot. He was proud of the expressionless mechanoid.

"The pod has not landed yet," said the robot.

The comment caught Tom by surprise. He had come to recognize the robot's "moods" by the way

74

he phrased things. It was not like him to be negative.

Tom's thoughts were interrupted by Dr. Friedman's shouts.

"I see her," he said pointing skyward. "Here she comes!"

Tom knew something was wrong. The pod was coming in too fast. "Signal the pod to abort the landing and try again," he said to the robot.

"Transmitting," said Aristotle. "My signal has not been received, Tom."

The pod sped by overhead, angling toward the icy surface of Ganymede. Seconds later, they saw ice and rock explode skyward.

Tom turned to Aristotle. "You did the best you could," he said.

"But I am, after all, a flawed mechanism," said the robot.

CHAPTER EIGHT

"Try veering left," said Ben.

Tom Swift turned the large thick steering wheel of the surface rover counter-clockwise. The rover responded sluggishly and Tom had to fight the wheel to get it to go a few degrees to the left of their present course, over the rough ice-covered surface of Ganymede. "What does the detector read now?" he asked, without taking his eyes from the terrain ahead.

"There's a slight change in the rate of the light's pulsations," answered the computer tech. "They're definitely faster."

"Try going more to the left," said Anita. She was sitting in the back seat of the rover, next to the robot. "According to what you saw, the equipment pod can't be too far away, Tom."

"I'm getting a confused sonarscan reading, Tom," said Aristotle. "I think my signals are bouncing off some very rough surface formations ahead of us."

"Thanks, Aristotle," said Tom. "Keep scanning, anyway."

"Thanks for volunteering us for this mission, Tom," said Anita. "I needed a break from the labour camp! I swear that if I have to spread one more tank of dome foam, I'll go nuts!"

The young inventor laughed. It sounded harsh through the suit radio. "I hate it, too," he said. "Unfortunately, thanks to the crash landing of pod number four, we may have one less dome to construct. As much as I dislike the hard work, I hope, for the Friedmans' sake, some of their stuff survived."

"What will the Friedmans do if all their equipment was destroyed?" asked Ben.

"They'll be able to carry on some of their experiments," said Tom, "but the expedition will pretty much be a disaster for them. They can do some short-range observation, and that's about all."

"We also won't know what happened to the Argus Probe, will we," said Anita. It was a statement, not a question.

"That's right," said Tom. "They had quite a series of experiments planned for Io and the 'flux tube'."

"The 'flux tube' is that weird magnetic effect between Io and Jupiter, isn't it?" asked Ben.

"Yes," said Tom. "Doctor Friedman—Fiona— said she was sure the equipment could have been used to locate Argus. It's a shame that we couldn't have carried it in the cargo hold of the *Daniel Boone*, but there was just too much stuff we *had* to carry."

"The signal is getting stronger," said Ben. "We're getting very close."

Tom looked out as far as he could see in the distance. There was no sign of wreckage.

"I strongly suggest that we reduce our speed, Tom," said Aristotle. "I don't like the readings I'm getting here."

Tom eased off the accelerator pedal and the compact electric vehicle slowed down. The ride *had* been getting rougher and rougher as the three young people and the robot followed the detector's signal.

Tom looked up at the great disc filling the sky on all sides, the planet Jupiter. He could see the Great Red Spot, that huge atmospheric storm that had lasted for hundreds of years. The expedition had hoped to discover new information about it. They would still go home knowing more than anyone had before the expedition, but...

"Look out," yelled Anita.

Tom felt the rover dip out from under him and there was a sudden sensation of falling. The rover had gone over the edge of one of the many sulci that had been found in the area.

As the rover slid over the edge of the big ice crevasse and started sliding down the deep side, Tom did his best to stay in the rover. He hoped Anita and Ben were doing the same. If they could stay with the wildly bucking little machine, they had less chance of being thrown out and possibly crushed, or getting a puncture in their suits. Tom was not worried about Aristotle, as he was not as delicate as the humans.

They hit the bottom of the sulci hard and the rover bounced three times before Tom wrestled it under control. "Was anyone hurt?" he asked anxiously. "I didn't see that dip!"

"Neither did I," said Anita. She didn't appear to be hurt, just a little shook up.

"I'm okay, Tom," said Ben.

The young people checked the robot for damage, but Aristotle had gripped the sides of the rover with his hydraulic hands and had managed to stay in, despite the roughness of the trip down into the sulci. Ganymede was full of surprises.

"We're very close," said Ben, excitedly. "The indicator light is blinking like crazy!" The young man got out of the rover and did a slow turn, watching the detector. "This way," he said, and started walking. He kept his eyes on the detector.

Tom looked around the bleak icy surface. Why didn't he see any wreckage?

"There should be parts and equipment scattered over the crash site and I don't see anything," he told Anita and Aristotle. "I guess we'll just have to follow Ben!"

When the rover caught up to him, Ben got in. "How much air do we have with us?" he asked.

"Another three hours for each of us," said Tom.

"Good," said Ben, "because according to the detector, we're right on top of the wreckage and I don't see a thing! We'll have to make a thorough search of this area!"

Tom looked around. The terrain was different to what they had been travelling over, but there was nothing unusual about it. "Spread out," he said, "but don't go out of sight of the rover."

The three young people loped off in different directions. The robot, as usual, stayed within visual range of Tom.

Tom and the robot picked their way carefully around the spiky ice formations that covered the area. There were many theories about the surface structure of Ganymede and they all involved high-pressure ice physics. But the most baffling feature, to planetologists, had always been the type of formation that they were now exploring, the sulci. The pattern of these mysterious grooves seemed to suggest that in Ganymede's past, there had been a lot of tectonic activity—twisting, sliding, and stretching of surface material. Yet something was missing. There was no evidence of "new" surface material. There was just a solid blanket of ice.

"Tom!" The young inventor recognized Anita's voice. "I think I've..." The rest of her sentence was drowned in a sudden explosion of static. Tom Swift hurriedly adjusted the reception on his radio, trying to get her signal back.

"Anita, I'm getting too much static," he said. He hoped she could hear him. "There must be something wrong with your suit radio."

"What's going on?" That was Ben's voice.

"Something's wrong, Tom," said Aristotle.

Tom turned to look back in the direction he had seen Anita go. He cursed the limited visibility and the sense-deadening qualities of the space suits. "Anita?" he called out again. The young woman was nowhere to be seen! She had disappeared from the surface entirely!

"Anita's circuits are patterned on my memory,"

said Aristotle. The robot fell silent, but Tom knew that he was using every one of his sensors to try to locate Anita.

Tom saw Ben leaping toward him. He was using the light gravity to cover distance by bounding across the surface. "Where's Anita?" he asked anxiously.

"Slow down, Ben," said Tom, "if you fall, you'll tear your suit! We'll find her, don't worry."

But Tom *was* worried about his friend. How could she have disappeared without a trace?

"*Anita,*" he tried yelling through the static on the radio. There was no answer.

Without comment, Aristotle began moving slowly forward.

"My sonarscan indicates that the surface beyond me is not solid, Tom," said Aristotle. "We must look for signs of fresh breakage in the surface crust. I believe Anita may have fallen through!"

Tom looked at the surface of the sulci again. Aristotle's theory made sense. The crust *was* different here. In fact, it looked as though it had been subjected to tremendous heat, and then liquified, sometime in the ancient past. It had refrozen almost immediately, however, leaving meringue-like peaks over the area. If that were true, then some parts of the surface *would* be weaker than others.

Aristotle stopped. The robot scanned the area with his cameras and then turned his sensor frame toward Tom. "The surface may not support my weight beyond this point, Tom."

"Wait here, then," said the young inventor. "Ben, get the emergency cable and something to dig with out of the rover!"

82

"Right," said the young Indian. Tom saw him gallop off in that direction. Without waiting for Ben, Tom started walking forward, gingerly. He tested his weight on the surface before taking each step.

Suddenly, the icy surface broke beneath his cleated boot and he pitched forward onto his knees.

He had stumbled into an air pocket formation. But there was no air on Ganymede. At least there wasn't *now*. It was just too cold. Any atmospheric gases would be frozen. But what if his theory about the area of surface formations were true? What if the sudden heat had liberated the frozen gases just long enough for them to form pockets in the liquid ice? When the whole thing froze again, the atmospheric gases would be flash frozen again, too, but the air pockets would remain.

And what about Anita? He looked out over the expanse of barren, frozen surface in frustration. Was she hurt badly? Unconscious? There was no way of knowing. Tom's vital link with her, her suit radio, gave him nothing but useless static.

There was also the matter of Anita's air supply. Tom and Ben would be able to get fresh tanks from the rover. They would have to find her before her tank ran out.

Tom squinted hard, trying to see if he could spot any places where there might be a fresh surface disturbance. It was so dark. The shielded helmet visor tended to distort things a little, too. It was maddening.

Tom watched as Ben drove up in the rover, and motioned for him to stop.

83

"Stop there," the young inventor told his friend. "We can't risk losing the rover."

"At least we can light the area," said Ben. "There are some emergency work lights that run off the rover's batteries!"

"We'll have to use them sparingly, though," said Tom, getting a large roll of braided steel cable and a shovel out of the rover. "We have no way of recharging the batteries and we need the rover to get back to base camp."

Ben nodded in agreement and began setting up the work lights.

Abruptly, Aristotle began moving forward. Tom noticed that the robot was not travelling in a straight line, but instead, he was zig-zagging along the moon's rough surface.

"Follow us with the work lights, Ben," said Tom, and he began to walk in the robot's tracks.

"I'm using my sonarscan to find the solid ground," said the robot. "It will also tell me where the surface is weak. The last time I saw Anita, she was travelling in this direction."

Tom was glad he had the robot to be his eyes and ears on Ganymede. If an accident like this had happened on Earth, he would have heard the ground cave in under Anita, and his sight would not be limited by the helmet of a space suit. Out here, his own senses were cut off and deadened by his survival equipment.

Aristotle stopped suddenly, and stood in silence for a few seconds. Then he raised one arm and pointed to his right. Tom saw that the surface where the robot pointed was slightly raised and bubble-like, but it was hard to tell anything else in the darkness.

"I'm getting some unusual echoes from that formation, Tom," said the robot. "There are some solid metal objects beneath the surface...and something else. Anita is there. I know her circuits."

The area was suddenly flooded with light. Ben had been monitoring Tom's conversation with Aristotle, and had aimed the work lights there. In the harsh light, the surface looked even more barren and alien. Tom tried to see as far as he could into the distance. Was the surface broken? He just couldn't tell. The static coming over his suit radio only fed his frustration. Anita could be buried forever under tonnes of ice, or she could be trying to dig her way out of a deep crevasse. Tom had no way of knowing.

"Direct me where the footing is solid, Aristotle," said Tom. "I'm going over there to investigate."

"How much do the objects you are carrying weigh, Tom?" asked the robot. "I must figure the extra weight into my calculations."

Tom hefted the cable. In the one-sixth gravity of Ganymede, there was really no way of telling how much it weighed. "There's about thirty metres of it," said Tom. "On earth, it would weigh about nine kilograms. Figure about three more kilogrammes for the shovel."

"You may proceed, Tom," said the robot "Go to the left of your present position for approximately five paces, then make a ninety-degree turn to the right."

Tom did as the robot directed. He began to notice a definite upward slope of the surface.

"Stop," he heard the robot say, a few moments later. "I suggest you test the surface very carefully with your shovel from here on, Tom," said Aristotle.

Using the shovel as a probe, Tom tested the ice one step at a time. It was painfully slow. He stabbed the shovel into the ice then took a step. Stabbed, then...

Suddenly, the ice gave way beneath him and he felt himself falling. It was a slow, tumbling kind of fall. He heard Ben's voice calling him anxiously all the way down.

"I'm sorry, Tom," he heard Aristotle say.

Tom Swift opened his eyes and looked up. A space-suited figure was bending over him. It was Anita. From his suit radio, he could hear Ben's frantic calls.

"Tom! Answer me, Tom," the young Indian was yelling.

"Everything's fine, Ben," said Tom. "I've found Anita and she's all right."

Tom could see Anita nodding her head, "yes", through her helmet visor. She pantomimed falling through the surface and then landing on her suit's transmitter. She made an "okay" sign with her gloved fingers. She could hear them, then. It must have been frightening for her to hear her friends trying to rescue her and to not be able to give them any help, Tom thought. He got up and put his arms around Anita in an awkward space-suited hug. He saw tears of relief rolling down her cheeks.

"I am pleased that you found Anita, and that both of you are all right," Tom and Anita heard

Aristotle say. "My errors caused these accidents. I would not blame you if you shut me down."

Anita looked at Tom with concern.

"*Aristotle*, will you *please* stop blaming yourself for everything that happens," said Tom, exasperated.

"I'm sorry, Tom," said the robot. Tom grimaced with annoyance. He was going to have to deal with the robot's inferiority complex very soon.

Anita made a wide gesture with her arms indicating their surroundings.

Tom could see that they had fallen into a huge underground ice cave. The sides were smooth, but the bottom was littered with rocks and chunks of ice…*and* pieces of equipment from pod number four. That's why they hadn't seen any wreckage. From the ground, it had been impossible to detect the presence of the cave. Tom knew it must be at least a kilometre in diameter, and hundreds of metres deep in some places. The whole area was probably littered with "bubble caves" of this kind.

"The pod's here," Tom said. "It looks pretty busted up, but there's no way of knowing if any of the equipment is still usable until we get it back to camp."

"We've got to get both of you some air pretty soon," said Ben. "My air level indicator just flipped over."

Tom saw Anita point to herself and nod her head vigorously. The suit indicators flipped from green to orange to show that the wearer had fifteen minutes of air left. When they went to red, that was it.

"There's more cable in the rover," said Tom,

"but unfortunately, I've got most of it down here. I'll have to get it to you somehow."

Tom Swift's mind usually worked very fast during a crisis, and this time was no exception. Within seconds, he had a plan.

"I'm going to try to toss you the end of my cable, Ben," said the young inventor. Tom looked around the floor of the cave. He needed to find something to weight the end of the cable with. He went over to the equipment pod wreckage and selected what looked like a heavy piece of twisted framework. That would do, he thought.

He unwrapped the cable and began winding the end of it around the piece of metal. Anita watched him, anxiously. Tom knew he would have to hurry. They didn't have much time left until their air ran out. Ben would have to lower the air tanks with the cable and it would have to be long enough to reach them. The delicate tanks would not survive being dropped.

When he was sure the cable was tied securely to the metal, he called to Ben. "I'm going to try tossing the cable out now. I just hope I can throw it high enough."

Had they been on Earth, Tom knew that there was no way he could have thrown the cable that high. But in one-sixth G, there was a chance his idea would work. He spun the end of the cable, for a minute, using the weight of the piece of metal to build up some momentum, and then he tossed it into the air with all of his strength. He and Anita watched it sail slowly upward, then fall back toward them. It had risen just short of the opening at the top of the ice cave.

"No go, that time, Ben," said Tom. "I'm going

to try again." This time, the young inventor jumped as high as he could into the air before flinging his arm back for the toss. It threw him off balance, but the cable went sailing out of the cave.

"I've got it," he heard Ben say. Anita jumped up and down, clapping her hands.

Tom watched the cable being drawn up through the hole, anxiously. His suit indicator flipped to orange. He glanced at Anita, anxiously. She must be almost out of air, he thought, but she's showing no sign of panic. She's an amazing woman, Tom thought, proudly.

Anita pointed to the top of the ice cave. An air tank, tied to the cable, was snaking down toward them. The two young people stepped back to avoid the pieces of ice that were being broken off by the cable.

"Easy, Ben," said Tom when the air tank was nearing the floor of the ice cave. As soon as he could reach it, the young man quickly untied the tank. He took it over to Anita and exchanged it for her empty one, then he tied the empty tank to the cable and said, "Take it up, Ben." Even though the tank was empty, it was valuable. Back at base camp, it would be refilled and used again. A few seconds later, Tom watched as Ben lowered the second tank to them.

After Tom's empty tank had been sent up, he and Anita looked around at the scattered pieces of the equipment pod.

"We've got to get as much of this stuff back to base camp as possible," he told the young woman. Anita nodded in agreement. Together, they began tying as much as they could to the cable and signalling Ben and Aristotle to haul it up. Presently, they were through.

"I've got to bring you both up now," said Ben. "We've got just enough air to make it back to camp."

Tom motioned to Anita to go first. She was reluctant, but he was insistent and she finally gave in. Tom tied the cable securely around her. He was careful to make sure that it would not interfere with any of her life support systems.

"Take her up carefully," Tom said to Ben. "Help Ben pull Anita up, Aristotle," he added.

Tom watched as Anita was pulled up. When she had disappeared over the lip of the hole, Tom went back to what remained of the wreckage of the equipment pod and fished through it until he found something he had seen earlier. It was the twisted mass of the pod's electronic components. If he had the physical evidence, maybe he could prove to Aristotle that the pod's crash had not been his fault. He knew he had to do something, or the robot's self confidence would continue to deteriorate.

CHAPTER NINE

"Those ice caves were a great find, Tom," the young inventor heard someone say from behind him. He flipped himself around, using one of the stabilising bars hooked to the bulkhead, and saw Dr. Sung Vangumtorn waving at him from the *Daniel Boone*'s main lift, as the doors closed. The Thai planetologist and his team were on their way down to base camp with the last of their equipment. Their dome was finished and from now until the *Daniel Boone* left Jupiter for home, they would be conducting their experiments from *Ganymede Base*. Tom knew that they had already planned a trip out to the ice caves, those strange surface formations that had almost been a tomb for his friend, Anita.

At least some of the teams of scientists were

carrying on their work successfully. Tom was sorry that he could not say the same for the Friedmans' astronomy expedition.

Tom floated by the door to the lab and looked down the long deserted corridor of the ship. Now that they were in geosynchronous orbit around Ganymede, the crew had taken the spin off the ship and those remaining aboard had to alter their life styles for the weightless condition. There weren't many people left aboard beside the Navy crew, however. Now that *Ganymede Base* was close to completion, everyone, except the personnel necessary to maintain the big interplanetary ship, had moved down there. Everyone except the Friedmans, who had no place to go. Most of the construction material for their dome, and almost all of their equipment had been destroyed in the crash of their equipment pod. Tom, Ben, Anita and Aristotle were doing their best to help the family of astronomers examine the pieces of equipment that they had salvaged, but so far, they had found very little of it that could be of any use to the expedition. It was all he could do to keep them from sinking into a deep depression. He knew they felt like dead weight to the rest of the Jupiter expedition.

Tom floated through the hatch of the lab, but he stopped, puzzled, when he saw his friends and Aristotle, gathered around Ian Friedman. There was something bolted down on the work table in front of the young astronomer.

Anita looked up, and motioned to him excitedly. "Look what Ian put together last night," she said.

As Tom floated toward the group, he could see

that Ian had indeed gone without sleep for quite some time. He looked pale and worn, and there were dark circles under his eyes.

But he *was* smiling, proudly. On the work table in front of him, Tom saw the capsule belonging to one of the probes that the Friedmans had been planning to send to some other moons of Jupiter. Data from the cameras on those probes, plus results of the core samples that the devices were to have taken, would have composed much of the team's research. Somehow, Ian had been able to put *one* together out of the pieces of the other *six*.

"I don't know what good it did to put this thing together," said the young scientist. "There's no way to send it anywhere. This is just the instrument package. The propulsion part of it was destroyed. I—I just had to do *something!*"

Tom looked at the probe and then he looked out the window of the lab into space. The stars looked back at him. "Which probe was this?" he asked.

"Most of it is the Io instrument package," replied Ian, "but there are parts of Callisto and the Amalthea packages here, too."

"Do you think it will still function on Io?" said Tom.

"I don't know. There's not as much heat shielding on it now as there was on the original probe. It doesn't matter, the thing's not going anywhere!"

Ben looked at Tom with a mysterious smile on his face that made Anita look quickly from one to the other. "You've got an idea, haven't you, buddy?" said the computer tech. "I can hear the gears meshing in your brain!"

Ian looked at the three friends, frowning in

puzzlement. "What's going on?" he asked anxiously.

"When I come back, I want you guys to have some ideas for heat shielding for the probe," said Tom. "I've got to go see a man about a ship! That means you, too, Aristotle," Tom said, looking straight at the robot's camera lenses.

Without another word, Tom left the lab and headed for the ship's lift. "Bridge," he said to the computer, as he pulled himself inside.

A few seconds later, he floated out onto the bridge. Two bored looking young crew members, with bands on their jumpers identifying them as "Ship Patrol" blocked his path.

"Identify yourself and state your business on the bridge," one of the SPs said, formally.

"I'm Tom Swift, Junior, and I'm here to speak to Captain Barrot," said Tom.

The SPs exchanged looks that Tom could not interpret, then one of them pushed off and floated toward a hatch that said "Navigation. Authorised Personnel Only" on it. The SP knocked on the hatch and said, "Mister Tom Swift, Junior, requests permission to see the Captain."

The hatch opened and Rafe Barrot stuck his head out. "Permission granted," he said, smiling. "Come on in, Tom!"

Tom pulled himself toward the hatch. "Thank you," he said as he passed the SP. The young man's face was an unreadable mask of formality. The military works in mysterious ways, Tom thought, as he entered the navigation room.

"It sure has been peaceful up here without all of the civilians," Barrot said, teasingly. Tom pulled himself into a seat beside Barrot and buckled himself in to keep from accidentally floating into the delicate equipment in the tiny room. There were switches, buttons, and digital read-outs all over it. Tom looked out of the view port and saw the surface of Ganymede framed by the planet Jupiter. It still thrilled him to look at it.

"How's it going?" Tom asked. He didn't want to come right out with a request for the lander and it really had been a long time since he had seen Rafe Barrot. He liked and respected the Captain very much.

"To tell you the truth, I'm bored stiff," said Barrot, laughing. "There's very little to do to maintain orbit and the regular Navy guys are driving me crazy with their 'spit and polish'! I'd really rather be down on the surface where all the action is. A Captain belongs on his ship, though!"

Tom nodded sympathetically. He knew that Barrot was the rugged adventurous type. That kind of person did not thrive under the burden of routine. Tom remembered all of the stories he had heard about Rafe and his friend, Martin Sanchez Nagayama, still Sergeant in the Army, and wondered how it was that Barrot had not gone "stir crazy", yet. He had met few people with more self-control than Barrot, however. That had to be the reason.

"What brings you up here, Tom?" asked Barrot, catching the young inventor by surprise.

"I need a ship," Tom said.

Barrot sat back in his chair and smiled at Tom. Tom could tell he had sparked the Captain's curiosity, however.

"Why do you need a ship?"

"I want to plant an instrument package on Io

and to find out what happened to the Argus Probe."

"You'll be wanting one of the long-range landing craft, then. Who's going with you?"

"Ben Walking Eagle, Anita Thorwald, and Aristotle, my robot."

"I can't let you be in charge of a Naval vessel, Tom. You'll have to let someone else be in charge of the ship."

"I understand, sir. Does that mean you're going to give me a ship?"

"Maybe. Your father is my friend, Tom, and what you're proposing to do is very dangerous, although it *is* something that pertains to the success of the Jupiter exploratory mission. I'd feel better if you had his permission. Have you talked to him yet?"

"No."

"If he says it's okay, then I don't see any reason why I shouldn't let you have a ship. You have more experience in space than most of the people on this ship and I know you know how to handle yourself. Let me see who's on the duty roster."

Barrot swivelled in his chair and faced a small CRT. He punched out a code on the miniature terminal and a list of names appeared. The last one was blinking. "Lieutenant Junior Grade Burt Foster is your man," said the Captain, smiling. "He's Navy all the way through so he'll expect a lot of formality from you. I wish I could go with you."

"I don't know how to thank you," said Tom.

"You still have to ask your father's permission," said Barrot.

Tom shook hands with the Captain and left the

bridge. Instead of going back to the lab, he got his space suit and went straight to the shuttle bay. He took the first lander bound for *Ganymede Base*. His father was waiting for him when he arrived.

"I got your message," said the elder Swift. "I'm very eager to know what is so important that it couldn't wait until the end of the work cycle!"

The two Swifts loped slowly across the short distance from the landing area to the airlock of the main dome in silence. The elder Swift cycled the lock and after a few seconds, they stepped from there into the decontamination shower.

As the liquid carried away the last traces of Jupiter's radiation, Tom organised his thoughts. The young man hated to think about giving a parent the "ol' hard sell", but getting the ship was important to him and it could mean everything for the Friedmans.

"Come with me," said Tom's father, when they had finished removing their suits.

The interior of the main dome was really a marvel. Every time Tom visited it, the work crew and the residents had made improvements on it to make it as comfortable as possible. The smaller domes weren't nearly as elegant. They wouldn't be, even when they were complete.

The dome had been divided into sections for living quarters, lab facilities, and common rooms. This had been done by erecting frame work panels and then spraying the panels with dome foam. The same principal had been used to create upper and lower levels by using the interior support structures as a base for building the upper levels.

The first level was actually below ground and it had been the first to be finished. The "human touch" had been added by the use of paint in warm colours on this level. Tom could see that the geometric design motif was spreading to the level above, too.

The elder Swift entered a cubicle and motioned for his son to follow.

"This is my living quarters, now. Make yourself at home."

Tom had to admit that his father's cubicle was very cosy. He wondered if the others were like it.

"I don't want to take up too much of your time, Dad," said Tom. "I know how busy you are. I just want your permission to take a ship to Io."

Tom's father looked at him in silence for a moment. When he spoke, Tom could hear the deep concern in his voice. "May I ask why you want to go to Io?"

"Ian Friedman was able to salvage one of the instrument packages from pod number four, but he's got no way to plant it. I want to see the Friedmans come out of this expedition with something, Dad, and besides, you know we've been wondering what happened to the Argus Probe. If I can find it, maybe I can fix it."

"You make it sound so simple," said the elder Swift, "but have you thought of the incredible danger involved?"

"Yes, but I've done dangerous things before, and you've never tried to stop me."

"I don't think I could if I tried, Tom. You're too much like me. It's not easy for me to see you go, though. You're my only son and I love you very much."

Tom swallowed hard. He knew what his father must be feeling. It would *never* be easy for him to see his son going out on a dangerous mission from which he might not return.

"You have good instincts, Tom," his father said, "and I know you know how to handle yourself in a crisis. Do you think this trip is really necessary?"

"Yes."

"I'll radio my permission to Rafe, then. Just be careful, son."

"I will, Dad. Thanks!"

CHAPTER TEN

The officer in charge of the *Daniel Boone*'s shuttle bay looked at Tom, Anita, Ben and the robot critically, for a moment. Then he looked at the CRT of his hand-held computerised activities roster. "You've been assigned to the *Meriwether Lewis*," he said. "She's on launch deck number two. Try to bring her back in one piece!"

"Uh…we sure will," said Tom, and he walked quickly past the man.

It was the period of full gravity on the *Daniel Boone* that the crew liked to refer to as the "spin cycle". Some muscle deterioration was expected among people who made their living in space. Those people had learned to schedule regular work-outs in a gym into their lives to combat what the lack of gravity did to their muscle tone. Because of the length of the Jupiter exploratory mission, however, *extra* care had been taken to give the passengers and crew as much time in full gravity as possible during the trip. Now that *Ganymede Base* was nearing completion, the spin cycles were the only chance anyone got to experience full gravity.

"He wasn't kidding," said Anita, when she, Tom, Ben and Aristotle were out of the officer's hearing range. "That's the trouble with being an empath..."

"A *what*?" said Ben.

"A human with the ability to read and share another being's emotions or feelings," said Aristotle.

"Aristotle has been helping me do some research on the subject," said the beautiful redhead, smiling at the robot affectionately.

"Aristotle has been helping you?" asked Tom.

"I asked him not to say anything to you about it until I told you," said Anita. "I was afraid you might think I was crazy, or something. I wanted some proof that empaths really exist."

"It was not a violation of my prime directive not to tell you, Tom," said Aristotle. "Had you asked me, I would have had to tell Anita's secret. Since you didn't ask..."

"I know," said Tom laughing. "I didn't ask you and therefore you didn't have to tell me!"

"Anita and I *have* shared current, you know," said the robot. "She is my friend."

"That makes you 'circuit brothers'," said Ben, teasingly.

"What?" said Anita.

"There's a custom among some Indian tribes

102

for friends to cut their fingers and let their blood mingle. The belief is that they'll be friends for life—'blood brothers'."

"When Mister Swift told me that the new microcomputer chip was affecting my nervous system, I became more aware of *how* it was affecting me. Now that I understand all of those crazy feelings I've been having, I can control them and even use them to my advantage," said Anita.

"That's how you were able to tell that the duty officer wasn't kidding," said Ben. "I bet all of the Navy people think we're going to wreck their ship and kill ourselves on this trip!"

"Yep," said Anita.

"No civilians are permitted in this area without clearance. Identify yourselves," a mocking voice said from behind them.

Tom whirled around in surprise and anger at being challenged so rudely. A young Naval officer, carrying a duffle bag, walked stiffly up to Tom and stopped.

"I said..."

"Just who are *you*?" asked Tom. He looked sternly down at the officer, who was at least a head shorter than he was.

"It doesn't work that way, Mister," replied the officer. "Now, before I call the SPs, who are you and why are you leading this 'freak parade' through an unauthorised section of a Naval vessel?"

"I'm Tom Swift and this is not a 'freak parade'! My friends and I *are* authorised to be here!" Tom showed the young man their passes. "We're going with the *Meriwether Lewis* on an exploratory mission to Io. We're the crew!"

"Oh no!" said the young officer. "Nobody told me about this. I'm not going anywhere with *this* crew!" The young officer brushed rudely by them and burst through the double doors marked "Launch Deck 2".

"I think that was Lieutenant Junior Grade Burt Foster," said Tom.

"He's going to be a great travelling companion," said Ben, sarcastically.

"He scares me, Tom," said Anita. Tom could see she was worried. "I don't understand why *you* can't pilot the ship!"

"The *Meriwether Lewis* is officially a Naval vessel, although Swift Enterprises designed and built her. I'm not in the Navy. We can't go without Lieutenant Foster so we've got to learn to ignore him. Let's get to the ship and get out of here! I'm excited about getting out into space again. *Ganymede Base* is interesting, but I guess I've got 'wandering fever' or something!"

"I'm with you, Tom," said Aristotle. The robot's remark surprised and amused everyone. They were still joking with Aristotle as they passed through the doors of the launch deck, but their laughter died immediately when they saw the resentful look on the young Lieutenant's face as he watched them approach the ship.

Tom walked up to Foster smiling, even though the young Lieutenant stared at him with undisguised hostility. "I think we got off to a bad start," the young inventor said. He tried not to make his friendliness look like an effort, but it really was. There appeared to be nothing likable about Foster. "Let's put our personal differences aside for the good of this mission, okay?" Tom said.

"Our differences aren't *personal*, Mister Swift," said Foster, coolly. "They're professional! Any time a civilian can..." Abruptly, Foster clicked his heels together and saluted. Tom turned to see Rafe Barrot walking toward them.

The Captain was smiling as he approached the group of young people, but Tom could see that there was a little tension behind the smile. Did it have something to do with Foster's complaints about him and his friends? Tom figured that Foster had talked to a superior officer after their first encounter, on the way to the launch deck. Had the complaints got as far as the Captain's ear so quickly? It was almost unheard of for the captain of a ship like the *Daniel Boone* personally to send off a tiny expedition like this one—unless he thought something might be wrong.

Barrot returned Foster's salute. "At ease, Lieutenant," he said. Tom noticed that Foster shifted to the proper military stance with crisp precision. The young Lieutenant was, however, far from being "at ease". Tom was not sure, but he thought that Rafe Barrot had noticed it, too.

The Captain smiled at Tom, Ben and Anita. "I wanted to make sure that you got off to a good start." He turned to Foster and, in a deceptively casual tone of voice, said, "You're not flying this ship all by yourself, you know! Tom, here, has logged a lot of time in space and he's an excellent pilot. I want you to listen to him if he has any suggestions, Lieutenant!"

"Yes, sir," said Foster. Tom noted that the

young Lieutenant was sharp enough to know that he'd been given an order. It had just been tactfully phrased to save him from embarrassment because of his earlier protests.

CHAPTER ELEVEN

"Will you come with me to check the cargo, Tom?" asked Aristotle. Tom was sitting in the co-pilot's couch on the bridge of the *Meriwether Lewis*. He swivelled around and looked at the robot questioningly for a moment, then he unbuckled his restraining harness and floated free of the form-fitting couch. The ship had just passed the lightly orange-hued moon, Europa, the second closest of the Galilean moons to Jupiter and the now unobstructed view of the giant planet caught Tom's attention for a moment. He would be needed on the bridge when they got closer to it and began their orbital descent, but he could leave his station for a little while, at least.

"Permission to check the equipment package,"

said Tom. Foster had insisted on this kind of formality from his "crew".

Foster, sitting next to Tom, in the pilot's couch, did not even look up. He seemed to be occupied with the navigation instruments. "Permission granted," he mumbled.

Tom left the bridge with a sigh of relief. He kept pace with the robot by pulling himself along with the hand-holds built into the ship. The *Meriwether Lewis* did not have the "luxury option" of being able to produce an artificial gravity like the *Daniel Boone*. Aristotle was using his motorframe as an electromagnet so that he would not float in the zero gravity of deep space.

Tom waved "hello" to Ben and Anita as he and the robot passed them in the corridor separating the bridge from the rest of the ship. Normally, they would have stopped to chat excitedly about the expedition and talk about plans for exploring the surface of Io, but Foster's attitude discouraged conversation. Anita smiled at Tom nervously as she passed. The young inventor could almost feel the tension that Foster had created on the ship. He knew Anita *was* feeling it.

"Why don't you shut down for a while," Tom said, gently putting a hand on Anita's shoulder as she floated near him. "You don't need to walk in zero 'G' and with your computer off, you won't be so sensitive to everything that's going on."

"That's a good idea," said Anita. Tom could hear the emotional fatigue in her voice. The tension inside the *Meriwether Lewis* had taken its toll on all of them.

"I'll help you," Ben said to her. Then, the young

computer tech looked at Tom and Aristotle. "Is something up?" he asked.

"No," answered Tom, casually. "Aristotle and I are just going to check the cargo. I wanted to stretch my legs, anyway. I've been in the couch for hours and when we get close to rendezvous with Io, I'm going to have to be in it again for quite a while." Ben accepted the explanation without comment. "When you get back to the bridge, would you run a check on the computer-controlled exterior cameras?" Tom asked. "I promised the Friedmans that we'd get some good close-ups of Jupiter as well as Io."

"Sure," said Ben, "but hurry back, will you? It's awful being on the bridge with just Foster!" He and Anita continued along the narrow corridor, toward the bridge.

Tom looked after them for a moment. He had wanted to tell them that something *was* up, but it wouldn't do any good to alarm them before he talked to Aristotle. The robot was disturbed about something, Tom knew that for sure. Aristotle was perfectly capable of checking the cargo himself.

They entered the cargo room and Tom shut the hatch behind them and locked it. "Okay, what's wrong?" he asked the robot.

"I have been communicating with the navigation section of the ship's computer, Tom. It is a relatively low-order intelligence, but sometimes I just need to talk to another machine. I hope you understand. Anyway, I was curious about our course, so I asked for details. Have you checked Lieutenant Foster's calculations?"

"No. I've tried to ask questions and make suggestions to him, but every time I do, he acts like

I'm plotting *mutiny* or something! Have you noticed all the 'busy work' he's been assigning just to keep all of us occupied and off his neck? He's suspicious of us, all right. I'm his main target, though. He won't tell *me* anything! What did you find out?"

"We are in grave danger. Lieutenant Foster plotted a course to Io that will take us quite close to Jupiter. In my estimation *too* close, Tom. We need an immediate course correction to keep us well out from Jupiter."

"We are going tangental to Jupiter? Like someone cutting across a lawn to get to the pavement?"

"Checking...Yes, I believe that illustration is essentially correct. It is my considered opinion, Tom, that Lieutenant Foster is not a sufficiently expert pilot to complete the course without danger."

"Oh, boy..."

"In addition, his plotted course indicates an attempted landing on Io without taking the precaution of orbiting Io to ensure sufficient deceleration for landing or identifying a proper landing site."

"In short, he's going to prove he's a hot-shot pilot by throwing out every safety precaution in the book!" said Tom. "He doesn't even care if the *Meriwether Lewis* is capable of that kind of handling!"

Tom always liked to get the "feel" of any ship he was piloting, so he had checked out the *Meriwether Lewis* as thoroughly as possible, without arousing Foster's suspicion. She was a fusion drive ship, like the *Daniel Boone*, but her design was totally different. She was, in reality, a short-range scout ship that had been developed by Swift Enterprises for fast runs to the space colonies and Armstrong Moon Base. She was sleek and streamlined, for entry into planetary atmospheres, and capable of remarkable manoeuvrability *in the right hands*. Until now, it had only depressed Tom to watch Foster handle the supple ship with little respect and a heavy hand. Now, it frightened him to death! Foster had to be stopped. But how?

"You must do something soon, Tom," said Aristotle.

"I guess this is where I test out whether or not the Lieutenant is going to follow Rafe Barrot's advice about listening to me."

"I predict he will not, but you must try."

"How was the cargo?" Foster asked, as Tom and Aristotle came back to the bridge.

Tom pulled himself down into his couch and connected the restraining harness. "The equipment package is riding fine," he said. "Why don't you take a break and let me run the ship for a while, Lieutenant?" He hoped his suggestion sounded very "matter of fact", but he saw anger flare up in Foster's eyes. He was sure Ben and Anita had seen it, too.

"That won't be necessary," Foster said coldly.

Tom decided to try another approach. "Have you run a computer simulation of our course yet? Maybe we should do that." That would give Foster a chance to change his mind if he wanted to and correct his calculations without being directly challenged by Tom.

"Let me worry about that," the Lieutenant said, tensely. It was obvious, Foster had taken the comment as a challenge. Subtlety was not going to work.

"All right, Lieutenant," said Tom, "Aristotle thinks your course is very risky. I trust him and I want to know what you're trying to prove by endangering all of us!"

To Tom's surprise, Foster leaned back in his couch and smiled. "I'm not endangering us, I'm saving a lot of time, that's all. Why don't all of you civilians relax and do a little sight-seeing. Leave the piloting to me."

"If I do that, we'll all be killed!" Tom exploded, angrily. "Why won't you listen to reason? You're so bothered by me being a civilian that you're willing to sacrifice our lives to prove you're a better pilot than I am and that's stupid!"

Foster's smile disappeared. "I won't tolerate insubordination on my ship, Mister."

"What are you going to do, make me walk the plank, Captain Blackbeard? You were ordered to let me help you but you've insisted on running the whole show yourself! That was fine with me until *now*! Now you're going to kill us and I'm not going to let you do it!"

"Consider yourself under arrest!"

"You're crazy, Foster!"

"You bet I'm crazy—crazy for accepting an assignment to play galactic chauffeur for a bunch of civilians! I'm the laughing stock of the *Daniel Boone*!"

"Only in your mind, Foster," said Tom. "I know that some of the officers aboard the *Daniel Boone* think that the Navy people are too good to associate with the civilians, but you guys forgot one

112

important fact. *Civilians* designed and built these 'Navy' ships you're so proud of!"

"Gentlemen," interrupted Aristotle, "I strongly suggest that you make your course correction *now* and settle your disagreement later."

The sharpness of the robot's tone made Tom look up. Chills ran up and down his spine. The bands of colour that made up the only *visible* surface of Jupiter were losing their definition. There was no longer such a sharp dividing line between the bands. One seemed to flow into the one next to it and they were taking on the characteristics of air currents, swirling into one another.

"The course stands as plotted," said Foster.

"This is *crazy*," shouted Anita. "Tom, can't you take over the ship or something? He's...he's out of his mind!"

"If one of you makes a move to do that, I'll kill you! It's my right as Captain of this vessel, under the circumstances!"

No-one moved.

"*Meriwether Lewis*, this is the *Daniel Boone*. Come in! Are you in distress?"

Foster jumped at the sound of the radio as if he'd been stung. It was apparent to Tom that the Lieutenant had forgotten everything except his hatred for everyone else on board ship.

But someone was keeping tabs on them.

Rafe Barrot?

Foster lunged at the radio. "We are beginning the final phase of the approach to Io. We are *not* in distress. Repeat. We are *not* in distress!"

"*Meriwether Lewis*, we are tracking your course and it is not—"

"*Meriwether Lewis* cutting transmission now,"

Foster snapped. Tom saw a flash of fear on his face for the first time. "We will resume communication when the Io landing is completed." Before the *Daniel Boone* could answer, Foster switched off the communicator.

Foster turned back to Tom and his smile returned. Tom noticed that it was a forced smile, however. "When they held that Three-corner race that you won, I had just been assigned to the *Daniel Boone* in preparation for the Jupiter expedition. The Navy wouldn't give me the leave of absence I needed to enter the race. Now you're going to see who would have won, Mister Swift! All hands to your stations! Prepare for Jupiter flyby."

"Foster," Tom said in a tight voice. "You're going to take us in too *close*! The gravitational pull is too much!"

"Afraid, Swift?" sneered Foster, his hostility quite open.

"Only crazy people aren't afraid," Tom said and knew at once by Foster's look he had made a terrible error.

Foster's fingers stabbed at the settings, changing the course still more, to direct the fast little ship even closer to the immense planet.

"No way!" shouted Ben, launching himself at Foster. His arms were outstretched, aiming for the Lieutenant's throat. In the zero gravity, he literally flew across the bridge.

"Don't do it, Ben!" Tom yelled. The young inventor jumped into the air and used his body to block Ben's attack.

Ben did a backflip and spun away from Tom. "Why did you stop me?" he asked angrily, as he grasped a bulkhead hand-hold. He turned his body expertly just as Tom had seen him do dozens of times in their games of null-gravity handball, and prepared to launch himself at Foster again.

"I stopped you because mutiny is still a crime punishable by death!" Tom snapped. "We may be civilians but we're under naval orders."

"But the alternative is to let this jerk run the ship right into Jupiter!"

"There are *always* other alternatives," said Tom. "Please, Ben. Let me handle this *my* way!"

"You've been given your orders," shouted Foster, "snap to it!"

Tom looked at Ben questioningly.

"All right," said the young computer tech, "we'll do it *your* way!" He floated over to a seat next to Anita and strapped himself in without saying anything. Anita looked at him worriedly, but also said nothing. There was nothing to say.

Tom felt a sense of relief but it was mixed with the same feeling of helpless frustration that he knew Ben had given in to.

"I could be in error, Tom," Aristotle said. "I am a flawed mechanism."

"In a few minutes, we may find out if you're right about that," Tom said, quietly.

"I hope that I am," said the robot.

Despite the filtering compound in the glassite viewport, the light in the bridge began to take on an orange tint which deepened rapidly. They were approaching the Great Red Spot, the single largest storm in the entire solar system. The sight was almost hypnotic. While those in the ship could not see any real movement in the Spot as a whole, they could see little wisps of curling storms and knew that each of those "minor" storms was almost as large as Earth itself. It was an awesome sight, looking down through the pit-like swirl in the thick, banded atmosphere of the great planet. Tom knew that had Jupiter only a relatively small amount of more matter it would have become a sun and the Solar system would have been a double-star, or binary, system.

Tom tore his eyes from the sight and looked at Foster. The tense young officer's fingers were busy, moving over the blinking controls of the ships. Beads of perspiration glistened on his forehead.

"Use the attitude engines," Tom said harshly. "Give it every bit of speed you can—*get us out of here*!"

"Shut up!" yelled Foster, but Tom noticed that one hand went toward the controls of the liquid fuel engines that served as the main guidance system for the *Meriwether Lewis*. Tom could tell that Foster was a man torn in half by his emotions. Part of him wanted to be practical and cautious, and part of him wanted to prove his superiority. Soon, it wouldn't matter which half won.

Foster fired the starboard attitude engines. The Great Red Spot shifted, slightly.

"Give it everything we have!" Tom said, making no attempt to hide the urgency in his voice. The view out the ports had become hazy, as if they were entering a great orange cloud. They had penetrated the atmosphere of Jupiter!

Tom looked at the radar screens, but they showed nothing much. At least they weren't going

116

to run into anything flying around out there, Tom thought.

The cloud thickened into an orange fog and almost simultaneously the ship began to quiver. The shakes became bucks as the ship fought the gravity and the turbulence of the Great Red Spot's eternal storms. The vessel twisted back and forth, then rolled hard to starboard. Foster snarled as he fought to bring the ship back under control. Tom realized Foster had lost orientation as he fired the attitude jets that pushed the ship inward, not outward. The ship screamed as the tortured metal was bent. It was like being in a runaway amusement park ride.

"We're going through the Great Red Spot!" said Anita. "It's a gigantic storm!"

"Let me help you," Tom yelled at Foster. "You can't handle this by yourself anymore!"

"Not on your life," screamed Foster. "If you can't take it, that's just too bad!"

Tom grabbed for the vital controls of the ship. Foster hit him hard in the jaw. Tom was stunned by the blow, but he shook his head hard to shake off the pain and dizziness.

Then, two metal arms wrapped themselves around Lieutenant Foster, pinning his arms. Foster struggled to break free, but human flesh was no match for hydraulics.

"*Aristotle!*" shouted Tom.

"There is no legal precedent for court martialling a robot, Tom. You must take control of the ship if we are to survive."

"You'll all die for this!" yelled Foster. "I'll see that you do! Let me go!"

Tom grasped the controls of the ship. Could he

117

pull the *Meriwether Lewis* out of the grip of Jupiter in time? A thick slush that Tom knew had to be liquid hydrogen was already sticking to the glassite ports as they sped deeper and deeper into the atmosphere of the planet.

CHAPTER TWELVE

Tom closed everything out of his mind except himself and the ship. He had trained himself long ago to achieve total concentration at will. He had learned to block out anything if he wanted to— noise, bothersome people, bright lights...anything. As an inventor, Tom considered his concentration to be one of his most valuable tools.

He needed it now. There was no time for computer corrections or proper procedure. The *Meriwether Lewis* had to become part of him.

An extension of his body.

All around him Tom could feel and hear the cries of the tortured ship as it fought not only the gravity of Jupiter—three times that of Earth—but the ripping, tearing winds. This craft—indeed few if *any* ships—had been designed for such stress.

Tom thrust forward the fusion engine accel
erator and at the same time gave the attitude en
gines full thrust away from Jupiter. He risked
quick look at the fuel gauge for the attitude en
gines: alarmingly low! They may lose the abilit
for finely-tuned flying later on, but if they lost thi
one, there would be *no* later on.

Outside, the atmosphere had deepened to slu
shy burnt orange fog. How deep was the atmo
sphere of Jupiter? Whatever it was Tom did no
want to find out first hand. The very weight o
the hundreds of kilometres of gasses would crush
their fragile vessel like an eggshell.

Tom was flying "by the seat of his pants", b
that set of senses which all born pilots possess. I
"seemed right" that Jupiter was *that* way and es
cape was *that* way. On this nebulous "feeling" Tom
was betting not only his own life but that of the
crew.

The attitude engines were located in severa
strategic positions around and under the *Meri
wether Lewis*. They were basically standard rocke
engines that had evolved to their limit, technically
Normally, they would be used to nudge the ship
gently into position for docking with another ves
sel, to provide braking action for landings on plan
etary surfaces, or to aid in course corrections.

The build-up of the G-forces was beginning to
tear at the ship and its passengers even more. I
took all of Tom's strength to keep his hands or
the controls, and he felt as if two huge hands were
crushing his head.

Tom fought the dizziness that threatened to
steal his consciousness. If he blacked out now, the
ship would go out of control and be lost.

120

The fusion drive was at full power and he could feel the vibration of the attitude engines. The fusion was pushing them *through* the thick atmosphere and the jets were pushing them *out*.

The G-force pushed him hard into the couch and he could hear Ben and Anita groan and Foster grunt. It felt as if the air was being pressed out of his lungs and the blood was draining from his brain. He saw spots of fuzzy blackness and the edges of his awareness seemed to blur.

But he felt a lessening...

The ship still tossed about like a twig on a stormy sea, but Tom knew that they had beaten Jupiter!

Tom and his friends were still breathing hard when he heard Foster's growl. "You think you're so smart, Tom Swift! If we get out of this alive, I'll..." A chocked noise of frustrated anger finished the sentence.

The orange soup became fog, then quickly thinned. They could see stars!

"Ben, contact the *Daniel Boone* and outline our situation. It won't do much good, but they should know what's going on, here," said Tom, ignoring Foster's threats.

"With *pleasure*," said Ben.

"What are you going to tell them?" shouted Foster. "Probably a bunch of lies! They'll never believe *you*. They'll *know* you took over this ship by force! When we get back to the *Daniel Boone*, I'm going to file a full report and press charges!" Foster twisted his head around until he could see Aristotle. "I'm going to make sure that *you* are shut down, too!"

"Sticks and stones will break my bones," said the robot. Foster gave him a look of pure hatred.

"Where did you learn that?" asked Tom, amazed. "I don't remember programming any coloquialisms into your memory!"

"I try to keep an open sensorframe and absorb all the knowledge about humans that I can," answered Aristotle.

"I sure hope you don't learn *anything* from the Lieutenant," said Anita.

"Why you..."

"This is the *Daniel Boone* calling, *Meriwether Lewis*." It was Rafe Barrot's voice.

Tom reached for the com. "Captain Barrot..."

"They took over the ship!" screamed Foster, at the top of his lungs. "I'm being held hostage by the robot!" The veins in Foster's neck and in his temples bulged as he strained against Aristotle's hold.

"There's been a problem, Captain," said Tom. "I don't know how to explain it, but..."

"We received your report, Tom. Ben transmitted *everything*, including Lieutenant Foster's planned course. Under the circumstances, the Lieutenant should consider himself under arrest. Whether you confine him to his quarters, or allow him to function as a crew member is up to you, Tom. I am transferring the command of the *Meriwether Lewis* to you."

"But . . . but . . ." Foster sputtered.

"Don't make your situation worse by disobeying orders, Lieutenant," said Rafe Barrot. "Is the rest of your mission in jeopardy, Tom? Will you have to scrub it?"

"Negative, Captain," said Tom. "I'm lower on

attitude engine fuel than I'd like to be, but we'll make it."

"Carry on, then, but keep me posted on your progress."

"Captain Barrot?"

"Yes, Tom."

"We have a lot of . . . er . . . *unexpected* data on the atmosphere of Jupiter. The sensors and the exterior cameras were in operation the whole time. I'd like to transmit it so that the Friedmans can begin their analysis!"

Rafe Barrot chuckled. "At least something worthwhile came from your unscheduled pass! We're ready on this end, so transmit what you've got. Good luck, Tom."

"It's down *there*?" Anita asked in disbelief. The young redhead floated just behind Tim's couch, using it to anchor herself in front of the glassite viewport. She and Tom watched, fascinated, as the *Meriwether Lewis* cruised slowly above the hostile-looking surface of Io.

Tom nodded. "This is our third orbit of Io at low altitude. The ship's sensors indicate that the Argus probe *is* inside the crater of that dead volcano ahead of us." Tom twisted around in his couch to look at Ben Walking Eagle, who was bent over his computer terminal like an anxious mother hen. "When are the computer photographs from the first pass going to come through?" he asked.

"Any minute," said Ben, not looking up. "It takes a while to get a hard copy from our set-up."

"Art is a fragile thing that cannot be rushed," said Aristotle. The robot was standing beside Ben, helping him with the computer. Tom had the feeling that even though Aristotle was a machine, he was just as anxious to see the photos as the humans.

Tom looked back at the multi-coloured surface of the inner-most Galilean moon of Jupiter with a mixture of curiosity and dread.

In some places, it was flat and marbled with streaks of fiery red, sulphurous yellow, and carbon black—like Yellowstone National Park without trees. Mostly, however, it was swollen and broken by the huge cones of volcanoes, which rose like giant, infected sores from the tortured landscape. A few of the volcanoes, such as the one the ship was now heading towards, appeared to be dead. Their sides were blackened by ancient layers of hardened magma and no fountains of liquid rock spurted up from their mouths. The majority of the volcanoes, however, were streaked by glowing streams of molten lava running down their sides, red-hot and deadly. Tom was very careful to steer the *Meriwether Lewis* around their gaping craters filled with boiling liquid rock.

"Wait'll you see what the cameras got!" exclaimed Ben. "The photos are coming through now and the computer did a first-class job of putting them together!"

Anita floated over to where Ben and Aristotle were carefully taking the photos out of the computer's printer. "They're really spectacular!" she said.

"Hey you guys," said Tom, from the pilot's couch, "stop, 'ooo-ing and ah-ing' over them and let me see them, too! I can't exactly drop what I'm doing to come over there."

"Sorry," said Ben. He brought a small stack of

the photos to Tom and pointed to a curiously indistinct object which gave off a metallic reflection. "I'm sure that's the Argus Probe. This photo is from the first pass over the crater. It looks like we went right over it, just like the sensors said we did."

"That object sure doesn't look like the Argus Probe the way I remember it! It's the wrong shape," said Tom.

"The image could be distorted by the high radiation level," said Anita. "We *are* entering the flux tube."

The three young people and Aristotle watched as Jupiter became visible in the view port from around the edge of Io. At first, they had not known what to expect when they entered the area between the giant planet and Io, called "the flux tube" by scientists. It was a region of mysteriously high electro-magnetic energy and intense radio radiation. The only effect, however, had been a sudden jump in instrument readings.

There were various theories about the reason for the flux tube's existence and about its effects. The most prominent one gave the material composition of Jupiter and Io as the source of the effect. What would it be like to be on the surface of Io in this region? No-one knew.

Tom Swift and his crew would be the first to find out.

"You might be right about the flux tube affecting these photos," said Tom, "but the shape of this object still looks odd to me."

Ahead of them, the huge black cone of the dead volcano bulged up from the surface. Tom headed the ship directly for the mouth of it.

"That volcano was sure an unfortunate choice for the Argus Probe to make as a landing site," said Ben. "If it was active, you would have lost the probe for sure."

"I think Argus was fooled by the size of the crater, somehow," said Tom. "But that's the chance you always take when you send an instrument package someplace without a human along to observe things and make independent decisions. The package we're carrying will have a better chance, since we'll be placing it exactly where we want it. I have the spot all picked out, in fact. After we check out Argus, we'll launch it."

"We have to land inside the crater of the volcano, don't we," said Anita.

"I'm afraid so," said Tom. He noted the apprehension in her voice. There was cause for it. "If we don't, we'll have to do a lot of climbing and that would be even more dangerous. Our sensors indicate that the volcano is not active, so I don't think there's much risk if we don't linger too long."

"I believe Lieutenant Foster is coming onto the bridge, Tom," said Aristotle.

Tom felt a twinge of guilt mixed with apprehension. Rafe Barrot had given him the choice of confining Foster to his quarters, or allowing him the freedom of the ship and Tom had taken the Lieutenant's word of honour that he would cause no further trouble. But Foster had been very withdrawn since his "arrest" and had spent most of the time in his cabin, leaving Tom to run the ship. He seldom spoke unless spoken to. Outwardly, he appeared calm, but Anita could not stand to be around him when she had her computer operating, so Tom knew that Foster was suppressing a lot of emotion. Had he learned his lesson after the near-fatal encounter with Jupiter? Tom wanted to think so. Anita, Ben and even Aristotle did not agree.

Foster pulled himself onto the bridge with the bulkhead hand-holds, and paused uncertainly.

"We're getting ready to touch down on the surface," Tom said to him. "I could use your help up here." The young inventor indicated the unoccupied co-pilot's couch, hoping that Foster didn't feel he was being patronised.

Foster merely shrugged and pulled himself into the couch without comment. It was a step in the right direction, anyway, Tom thought to himself.

Or was it?

CHAPTER THIRTEEN

Tom Swift cut the attitude engines and braced himself against the couch. A second later, the *Meriwether Lewis*'s landing supports contacted the surface of Io with a bone-jarring thud. The ship bounced twice on its shock absorbers and was still.

"Oh, do I feel *heavy*!" groaned Ben. The computer tech unsnapped his restraining harness and stood up with visible effort. Even though the gravity of Io was very close to that of the Earth's moon, their time in the weightless conditions of deep space had taken its toll on everyone's muscles.

"It's so quiet!" exclaimed Anita.

"It certainly is," said Tom. "You never realize how much noise there is in just the act of *existing* in a world where there is life until you get someplace like this. On Earth, there are always background noises—the movements of animals and insects, the wind, gurgling water. Even when it's 'quiet', the Earth is a pretty noisy place." The young inventor rose from his couch to stretch.

"*Tom...*" Aristotle said, loudly.

Tom turned, startled by the urgency in the robot's voice. The next moment, the deck of the *Meriwether Lewis* seemed to have been pulled out from under him and he fell to his knees. The entire ship began to shake violently.

"Moonquake!" yelled Foster.

"Everyone get down!" Tom ordered.

The instruments rattled in their housings and the very framework of the ship groaned with the force of the quake.

"I regret that I was unable to warn you sooner," said Aristotle. "My sensors picked up the quake only a moment before it happened. I suppose you could say that it crept up on me! Oh, how can you stand to have such a flawed mechanism like me around?" the robot finished, woefully.

The quake was over as suddenly as it had begun. Tom breathed a sigh of relief and got to his feet.

"I thought you said this volcano was *inactive!*" Foster shouted at Tom, angrily.

"*Ben?*" Tom asked, concerned. "*Is* the volcano going to erupt?"

"The sensors don't indicate it," said the young computer tech, "but I could be misinterpreting some of their data. I'm going to run some tests of my own just to make sure!"

Tom could tell that Ben was upset about the surprise quake.

Were they in danger?

"Io is volcanically active all over," said Anita.

130

"I'll bet the quakes are a frequent happening and normal. We'll just have to get used to them."

"If the instruments are to be trusted, you're right," said Tom. "Still..." He didn't finish the sentence. He didn't have to. The doubt had already been planted in everyone's mind.

"Ben, stay here and work on the quake problem," said Tom. "Aristotle will help you. I'll take Anita and Lieutenant Foster with me." Tom motioned to Anita and Burt Foster. "Let's suit up and take care of business so we can get out of here!"

"Good idea," said Anita.

Foster shrugged and said nothing.

Tom popped the hatch of the *Meriwether Lewis*'s airlock and felt the instant, mind-searing pain of intense, high-pitched bursts of radio static. He fumbled for the controls of his suit radio and shut it off. Anita had fallen to her knees, clasping her plexiglass helmet in a useless reflex gesture against the pain. Foster had collapsed and appeared to be unconscious.

Tom rushed over to Anita and shook her to get her attention, then motioned for her to turn off her suit radio. She reacted groggily but a moment later, Tom could see the relief on her face.

Tom and Anita shook Foster hard and somehow, managed to communicate the message to him. The three young people watched the ladder tumble down from the hatch to the surface of Io weakly.

They had to have suit radios.

Tom decided to try an experiment. He pulled in his suit radio's antenna all the way, then he thumbed the "high filter" button on his helmet up to full. Delicately, he switched on the suit radio with the volume at its lowest setting.

He winced as the bursts of static assaulted his now injured ear drums again, but this time, it was at a tolerable level. He motioned for Anita and Foster, who had been watching him, to do the same.

"What happened?" asked Anita. Tom could barely hear her through the static.

"The 'flux tube effect', I guess," Tom answered. "The radio radiation between Jupiter and Io is just too much for the suit radios. I'll have to make some modifications when we get back to the ship. Right now, I want to go take a look at Argus. We can travel with our radios off. Just give some kind of signal if you want to communicate and stay in sight."

Tom turned and backed carefully down the ladder. It was slow going because he had to make sure of each foothold with the clumsy boots and each grip with the thick shielded gloves.

Unexpectedly, he felt an attack of vertigo and paused on the ladder in an effort to control the sickening nausea that accompanied it. It would not be a good idea to throw up inside his space suit. The feeling alarmed him because in all the time he'd been flying, he had never felt vertigo, the sudden dizziness and loss of directional orientation.

Why now?

Tom looked up and instantly knew the answer. At the spot where he had paused on the ladder, he had cleared the ship. The striped face of Jupiter now occupied his vision totally, bigger than

132

he had ever seen it. The hazy atmosphere of the big gas giant dipped and swirled before his eyes. From his position on the ladder, he could not see space or the surface of Io.

Only the hypnotic atmosphere of Jupiter, a few hundred thousand kilometres away.

Tom looked down at the surface of Io and felt better.

Tom jumped from the last rung of the ladder to the surface. It was only a short jump, but he felt stabbing pains in his knees from contact with the solid lava rock floor of the volcano crater. He stepped to one side and steadied the ladder for Anita.

"Where is Argus?" the beautiful young redhead asked as she jumped down beside Tom.

"I didn't want to put the *Meriwether Lewis* down too close to it," Tom replied. "The heat from our landing probably wouldn't have affected it, but I didn't want to take any chances of destroying any physical evidence of what's causing it to malfunction."

"It looks like we're in for a hike, then," said Anita.

When Burt Foster was safely on the ground, the three young people set out to find the probe with an electronic locator Tom had attached to his suit's utility belt.

Ground that had looked smooth from hundreds of metres above the moon was, close up, quite rugged. Looking around, Tom could see how Argus's sensors could have been fooled by the size and geological formations of the crater. It was so vast, that it reminded him of the Great Salt Lake

133

Valley, in Utah—as it might have looked two million years ago, that is!

Tom moved uncomfortably in his suit. He could feel the sweat running down his back. It was difficult to get good footholds in the lava rock that had hardened, in most places, in intricate and convoluted flow patterns. Even in the one-sixth gravity of Io, the exertion of their hike was taking its toll on them.

Especially Anita. Although the beautiful redhead kept herself in the best physical condition possible, having to manipulate her artificial leg under these conditions appeared to Tom, to be difficult for her. He wondered whether her empathic powers were hampered by her thick lead-shielded space suit.

At this rate, they would use up their breathing mixture in a very short time. Tom wished they had a rover, but knew that the terrain of Io would have been too rough for any of the machines the expedition had brought. Machines were wonderfully convenient, at times, but they were more limited and less adaptable than man.

Even Aristotle had his limitations.

Tom checked the locator on his belt. The tiny light in the centre of it pulsed strongly. That meant they were getting close. Ahead of them, was a steep lava hill that they would have to climb or go around. Tom signalled a halt and indicated that Foster and Anita should turn on their suit radios.

"Ten minute rest stop," he said through the maddening static.

"I could use it," he heard Anita say. He watched as she checked the ground for sharp stones that could puncture her suit and then sank down gratefully.

Foster, on the other hand, stood, stubborn and defiant. "We're wasting ten minutes of air," he argued. "If Ms Thorwald can't take the pace, she should go back to the ship!"

"Take ten minutes, Lieutenant," said Tom, "that's an order. I don't care how you use it, but I'd advise you to sit down and rest while I decide where we should go from here!"

Foster made an obvious show of switching off his suit radio and then, to Tom's surprise, began to climb the hill, not looking back.

That was the first order Tom had seen Burt Foster openly disobey. Did it mean the Lieutenant's self-discipline was breaking down? Tom hoped not. The only thing he could control Foster with was Foster himself—and with force.

Tom did not want to use force.

"Ship to shore party!" Ben's urgent voice broke into Tom's thoughts. "Mayday! Mayday! Brace yourselves for another moonquake! Aristotle says..."

Tom did not wait for him to finish, but flattened himself onto the rocky surface. Anita did the same. They both looked in the direction that Foster had gone and saw him on the hill above them.

He had not heard Ben's warning.

Tom felt a vibration coming from deep inside the surface and tensed his muscles for the coming shock.

It was as though Io was having a violent convulsion.

Anita screamed as bits of rock began to pelt their suits, rolling down from above.

135

Tom looked up to see Burt Foster sliding down the hill toward them very fast and totally out of control.

One tiny hole in his space suit and Foster's blood would boil in the vacuum of space.

"We've got to try to catch him," Tom shouted to Anita.

"I'll try," she answered. "I hope he's not heavy, though!"

Tom could see that Foster was trying to grab a handhold on the rock as he slid down, but he was sliding too fast. Tom winced as small rocks pelted him, broken off by Foster's desperate effort to stop his fall.

"Brace yourself, Anita," Tom called out. "We'll have to use our bodies to break his fall!"

"I always loved tackle football," was her answer.

"Here he comes," shouted Tom. "Grab him!"

Tom and Anita grabbed for handholds on Foster's suit while trying to keep from being dragged down with him.

They couldn't hold him.

Anita let go first, and clawed desperately to keep her hold on the shaking surface of the crater.

"I'm sorry!" she wailed.

Foster's weight was too much for Tom. He felt helpless as the Lieutenant slid by him.

Tom whipped his body around to try to catch hold of Foster again and a sickening feeling of fear stabbed at his guts as the fabric of the man's space suit slipped through his clumsy gloved hands.

Then he saw it.

The moonquake had cracked open the surface. A yawning chasm, of a size that could swallow them all *and* take the *Meriwether Lewis* for dessert gaped below where he and Anita were desperately clinging. Foster would slide right into it if he couldn't stop himself.

Tom tried to get up, but he couldn't keep his balance. The heaving surface threw him back down again.

Hard.

He watched Foster, helplessly.

The young Lieutenant's legs went over the side of the split and Tom saw him make a last desperate attempt to stop himself by grabbing at the lava rock.

Foster's grip held. His legs dangled into the huge rip in the surface of the crater, but as long as he could hold on, he would not fall in.

Looking past Foster, Tom could see the *Meriwether Lewis* swaying on her shock absorbing landing legs. He wondered how Ben and Aristotle were handling the quake.

They had to get away from here!

Tom felt a lessening in the quake's intensity. He hoped it would be enough to allow him to get to Foster.

"I'm going to try and get him," he said to Anita.

"I'll go with you!" she responded.

"No, you might get hurt."

"*Please*, Tom. You may need my help."

Tom had to admit she was right. The days of the helpless heroine were gone, all right. "Follow me," he said.

Tom and Anita were able to stand and keep their balance enough even though the surface under them trembled. They reached Foster quickly. It was a simple matter to pull him off the edge of the chasm. Tom chanced a look down and gulped when he couldn't see the bottom.

As soon as he was on his feet, Foster struggled to break free of Tom and Anita. Instead of being grateful, Tom realized, with a shock, that the young Lieutenant was angry.

Foster switched on his suit radio. "Why did you two change your minds?" he asked. "You let me fall hoping I'd get killed so that you could invent some kind of cover story for Captain Barrot. But you lost your nerve at the last minute!"

"That's a lie!" Tom shouted into his radio. "You disobeyed orders by going up that hill alone and switching off your radio. We tried to catch you when you fell and you know it!"

Anita looked at the darkly handsome Foster through his helmet faceplate. "You're really twisted Foster!" she said contemptuously.

"Ship to shore party," Ben cut in, anxiously "Come in! What's going on out there?"

"It's nothing serious," said Tom, looking straight at Foster, who glared back at him. "Just a little disagreement. Thanks for the warning about the quake. I think it saved our lives."

"You can thank Aristotle for that," said Ben "I was busy waiting for the rest of the computer composite photos when he gave the warning. Are you guys coming back now?"

"I want to retrieve the probe, Ben," said Tom He looked questioningly at Anita.

"I'm going, too," she said.

"Foster?"

"I wouldn't miss a chance to see the great Tom

Swift swallowed by the volcano!" replied the young Lieutenant.

"I'm keeping the channel open from now on," said Ben. "I'll holler the minute I get something."

Tom turned and started back up the hill.

CHAPTER FOURTEEN

Tom, Anita, and Burt Foster stood at the top of the lava rock hill they had just climbed and looked, with disbelief, into the valley below them.

In the centre of it stood the Argus Probe and next to it—or rather, almost on top of it—hovered the strangest craft Tom had ever seen. It looked like a huge metal insect and it loomed over the Argus Probe as though that machine were its prey.

"Wh-what is it?" breathed Anita.

"It doesn't look like one of ours," said Foster. The Lieutenant seemed to have forgotten his personal hatred for Tom and Anita, for the moment. 'I would know if our military had that kind of design in the works."

The workings of the military mind could be amazing, sometimes, Tom thought to himself. It was such a simple thing to view the world in terms of "ours" and "theirs". It made decisions easy.

"What's going on?" Ben broke in. "What have you found?"

"Argus has company," answered Tom. "You'd better send Aristotle down here right away. I'm going to need him."

"I am on my way," came the robot's reply.

"Swift Enterprises hasn't got anything even remotely resembling that thing," Tom continued, thoughtfully. "How about the Luna Corporation? Could this be one of their long-range exploratory probes?"

Anita snorted in disgust at the mention of the second biggest multinational corporation next to Swift Enterprises. "If nobody has a design like that for a probe, then the Luna Corporation couldn't possibly have sent it up here. There was no one for David Luna to steal the design from!"

Tom had to admit that the probe did have a unique design. It consisted of three distinct parts. The head, shaped like an inverted tear-drop, contained two huge multi-faceted lenses and what looked like the same sort of sensing equipment that Aristotle had in his sensorframe. The head terminated in two powerful-looking metal pincers which appeared to be like mechanical hands, hydraulically operated.

The head was connected to the frame of the probe's exo-skeleton. What Tom knew had to be the brain of the probe was housed in the centre of the exo-skeleton. It was a smooth egg-shaped object with a sculptured handle moulded into it. The handle was obviously for installation and removal purposes.

Tom could see that the handle was built for a hand much like his own.

The probe's "legs" extended down from the mainframe. There were eight of them and they were jointed in several places. Again, Tom saw evidence of hydraulic operation. That meant that the probe must actually walk—when it had all of its pod-like "feet". Two of these seemed to be missing and two more looked twisted into unnatural positions. It was hard to tell from a distance.

"It could be an alien probe," said Tom.

"That's ridiculous!" said Foster. "The Navy has done studies on the possibilities of life in outer space and the odds are strictly *against* another life form like ours existing anywhere in the galaxy!"

"Why does it have to be a humanoid life form?" Tom asked. "Just look how many different life forms there are on the *Earth*. The possibilities are infinite."

"Those other life forms are vastly inferior to us," argued Foster. "None of them are capable of building and launching a space probe."

"That still doesn't prove anything, in my opinion," said Anita, "and I'm basing my statement on the evidence of that probe down there that's staring at us!"

As if to prove Anita's point, the strange probe cocked its head to one side as if it were questioning the behaviour of the alien beings watching it. The action reminded Tom of a Preying Mantis he had once seen in his garden at home. He had spent an hour watching it watch him and wondering what thoughts were passing through that insectile brain.

"You're right, Anita!" exclaimed Tom. "It knows we're here. It's 'aware'!"

"That makes it more of a robot than an actual 'probe' as we apply the term," said Ben over the radio. "It may be intelligent. I'd be careful."

"I'm going down there to have a closer look at it," said Tom.

"This is a top secret discovery," said Foster. There was a tone in his voice which Tom did not like. It had the hint of trouble in it. "I'm going with you as a representative of the United States Government."

"Why don't you just come right out and say that you're afraid we'll discover something down there that we'll immediately try to sell to 'the enemy', whoever that is?" Anita said angrily.

Foster glowered at her, but did not pursue the argument.

Quickly, but carefully, the three young people picked their way down the lava rock slope, their eyes on the probe. Its glittering, multi-faceted eyes watched them.

At the base of the slope, the ground levelled out. Tom, Anita, and Foster edged toward the probe slowly and deliberately from that point on. They did not want any of their actions to be interpreted as hostile.

When they were a hundred metres away from the probe, Tom called a halt. The young inventor was now able to judge the probe's size more accurately. It stood just a little taller than he was.

"The probe's legs are stuck in the rock!" exclaimed Foster. "It looks like the thing landed here when the volcano was still active and the lava solidified around it, trapping it!"

144

"The broken legs may be from its efforts to free itself," said Tom. "I wonder why Argus landed so close to it? Ben, I'm going to signal Argus to start transmitting data. If the cameras are still operative, the pictures might tell us something. Are you and the computer standing by to collect what it sends?"

"I'm set up, now," said the young computer tech, from the ship, "but the pictures from the second Io pass, over this volcano, are being assembled, so is it okay if I put the Argus data on hold for a while? I'm still trying to find out if we can expect an eruption any minute!"

"Sure," said Tom. "Stand by." He pressed a button on the locator he had used to track the probe. It sent an invisible tight-beam radio signal to the squat mechanoid. The hundred eyes of Argus—its sensors—began to glow in recognition.

Instantly, two ruby red beams shot from the eyes of the insect probe and converged centimetres away from Tom's boots. Tom jumped back, alarmed. The beams had burned into the lava rock as though it were plastic.

"It picked up my signal to Argus and it's warning me to keep my distance," said Tom. The young inventor knew that if the probe had wanted to kill him, he would now be quite dead. He shuddered involuntarily.

But why did the alien want him to stay away from Argus?

"The probe's signal is being blocked, Tom," said Ben.

"I know," said Tom, worriedly. "The alien probe seems to be holding it hostage."

"What?" asked the young computer tech. "Why…"

The rest of Ben's sentence was drowned out by a high-pitched screeching noise.

Suddenly, a bolt of visible energy shot from the surface of Jupiter like lightning and struck the crater's rocky surface. A shower of rock exploded into space, a few kilometres away.

The head of the alien probe swivelled around to follow the strange lightning.

The effect was over in seconds.

"What happened?" yelled Foster. Tom could tell the Lieutenant was really afraid. He had good reason to be. The bolt of energy could have struck them!

"It's part of the flux tube effect," said Tom. "For an unknown reason, those exchanges of visible energy happen frequently here. It may have to do with the cores of Jupiter and Io reacting to each other."

"It sure caused a lot of radio interference," said Ben.

"Look out!" screamed Anita. "It's going to shoot at us again!"

The probe's eyes seemed to glow angrily.

Tom knew they could not outrun the probe's beams. Why was it going to shoot at them?

Abruptly, the destructive light in the probe's eyes died and it seemed to look past them. Tom whirled around to see Aristotle coming toward them.

"It was just a misunderstanding, Tom," said the robot. "The alien thought you were trying to trick it. A similar energy phenomenon brought it here in search of intelligent life. When it arrived, it realized it had made a mistake and there was no life here, but not before it became trapped. I am glad that I intervened in time."

"You communicated with it?" asked Tom.

"Yes. The alien has analysed the programming of Argus and can communicate in binary."

"Has it come to destroy the Earth?" Foster asked excitedly.

"You've been watching too many science fiction movies, Lieutenant," commented Ben. "I'm glad you got there in time to prevent an accident, Aristotle."

"I am relieved that the alien did not destroy my creator," replied the robot.

CHAPTER FIFTEEN

"You called it 'the alien', Aristotle," said Tom.

"The probe is from the Alpha Centauri system. I think that qualifies it as 'alien'," said the robot.

"That's right here in our galaxy!" exclaimed Anita. "I always thought that if we had visitors from outer space, they'd be from another galaxy—like Andromeda, for example!"

"On the contrary," said Tom. "Think about the distances you're talking about when you use the term 'galaxy'. Our sun is just one dinky star in the whole Milky Way Galaxy. Alpha Centauri is just another dinky star. It happens to be our closest neighbour, sure, but it's still over one parsec from us. That's over three light years. If we could travel at the speed of light, we could make it there in about four years.

"The Andromeda galaxy, on the other hand, is two-million, two hundred thousand light years away. Any civilization that sent a probe from the Andromeda galaxy would be dead by the time it got half-way to us at light speed!

"We can now travel at one-tenth the speed of light with our present technology, fusion drive. Even at that rate, it would take us about four-hundred years to get to the people who sent this probe!"

"That probe travelled four-hundred years to get here?" asked Anita.

Tom looked at Aristotle questioningly. "*Has* it been travelling that long? And how long as it been stuck on Io?"

Aristotle was silent a moment. When he spoke, Tom was surprised. The robot sounded flustered.

"No, Tom. The alien has not been...travelling for that length of time. It will not tell me how long its journey was from its exact point of origin, however, it has been *here* a much longer time. One revolution of the striped gas giant—Jupiter—around its primary."

"That's twelve Earth years!" said Tom. "If it's been stuck on Io longer than the time it took getting here...the alien's civilization must have a star drive!"

"That is correct," continued Aristotle. "The alien is a messenger, but it will not divulge its message until the proper time. I do not understand its motives or purpose, but the message is of such importance that we must be deemed worthy to receive it. What criterion the alien will use to make this determination, I also do not know. It is an impatient and short-tempered mechanism,

Tom. That is due to its long entrapment and the urgency of its message. I am sorry I have failed to find out the scientific information you asked for."

"You haven't failed, Aristotle," said Tom. "After all, you *are* the only one who can talk to the alien. Is it *difficult* for you to talk to it?"

"Yes, Tom."

"Tom!"

"What is it, Ben?"

"I've just finished scanning the computer photos and we could be in serious trouble!"

"The volcano?" asked Anita, worriedly.

"Yep. I analysed the photos from our second pass and everything looked normal. Then I compared them to the photos from the first pass. There's a bulge that's growing bigger by the hour on the north side of the cone. That's an indication of a lot of pressure build-up under the surface! The frequency of the moonquakes is also an indication of that. I think the volcano is about to blow!"

"We've just made the scientific discovery of the century and we're about to lose it!" said Tom, frustrated.

"Tell the probe that I'm a representative of the United States Government and that I'm authorised to receive any message the probe might have. I am a Navy officer, you know!" said Foster to Aristotle.

"You can't do that!" said Anita. "You're only a Lieutenant and besides, you're officially under arrest!"

"I think you *all* better get back to the ship!" Ben said.

ve got to get Argus," said Tom.

"Argus can be of no further use to you, Tom. Its mind is gone," said Aristotle. There was a tone of sadness in the robot's voice. "Exposure to the probing of the alien was too much for its simple circuits."

"We could take the alien probe with us, but it won't let us get near it," said Tom. "Can't you find out its message?"

Suddenly, the ground beneath them began to shake.

"We have to go!" pleaded Anita.

The alien probe swayed on its spidery legs for a moment and was still.

"It was only a harmonic tremor," said Tom, relieved, "but another moonquake is sure to follow."

"The alien informs me that the events taking place resemble those that brought about its entrapment!" said Aristotle.

"I don't like this situation," said Ben, tensely.

"Aristotle, inform the alien that we want to take it with us," said Tom, "and that if it doesn't wish to go, it must tell us the message now because we're leaving!"

"The alien is not responding," said Aristotle.

"My air-level indicator just changed over, Tom," said Anita. "I've only got a few minutes left."

Suddenly, a flash of energy shot from Jupiter to Io. An explosion of rock marked its landing.

"Io *must* be some kind of ground for electrical energy generated in the atmosphere of Jupiter at certain times in its revolution," said Tom.

"And it triggers the volcano every twelve years," said Foster. "We can't leave it here, Tom!"

"If that's true, then the surface activity is only going to get worse," said Anita.

"If we can analyse the probe's star drive, we'll have the secret of interstellar travel! We could build the mightiest army in the galaxy!" yelled Foster. "Don't you understand what that would mean?"

"I understand that if we don't get out of here, we're all going to be fried!" said Tom. "Let's get out of here!"

"Look at the alien probe!" yelled Anita. "It's moving!"

The young people watched, as the alien probe applied all its hydraulic force to the trapped legs.

"Get back!" yelled Tom. "It's trying to break free of the lava rock!"

"It's not going to work!" said Anita dismayed.

The ground under them began to tremble.

"Get out of there, Buddy! The crater's breaking up!" shouted Ben.

"The volcano is erupting?" asked Foster.

"It looks that way," said Tom. "If we don't get out of here now, we'll get trapped like the alien...or worse! Head for the ship, everybody!"

Foster cast a last mournful glance at the alien probe, then he and Anita began running for the ship.

"Come on, Aristotle," said Tom.

"Wait!" cried the robot. "The alien is a messenger from beings who call themselves the Skree. It has come to search for help against...something it calls the Chutans—beings who are conducting a war of conquest against the Skree."

"*Come on*, Aristotle. There's no time left!" said Tom.

153

"No! It must not fail in its mission. The alien captured Argus reasoning that the beings who constructed that mechanoid would come after it. You came. The alien wishes to go with us!"

"I can't pull it out of the lava now," said Tom. "There's just no time!"

"The alien knows it cannot remain whole and fulfill its mission. It wants you to remove the memory core, Tom. It offers the secret of the star drive in exchange."

Tom was torn between the risk of survival and his scientific instincts. The alien made the choice simpler. Tom and Aristotle watched, fascinated, as the alien probe unlocked its egg-shaped brain core from its exo-skeleton.

"Unplug the sensor cables, Tom," urged Aristotle. "Hurry!"

Tom put his caution aside and approached the alien probe. It made no move to stop him. Reaching up, he unplugged all the cables he could see connecting the probe to the exo-skeleton. One by one, the probe's systems seemed to die.

Could a machine die?

It was truly as if the life force of the probe had suddenly gone out. Without the brain core, the strange craft was only a lifeless piece of hardware.

Tom lifted the core out of the exo-skeleton easily and cradled it in his arms.

"Head for the ship!" he shouted to Aristotle.

"Now that the alien's brain core is disconnected from its exo-skeleton, I can speak freely, Tom," said Aristotle. "It was difficult for me to communicate with it because its logic circuits have been under great stress from its long captivity on Io.

154

The probe is, to use a phrase applicable to humans, quite insane."

"What?" said Tom, alarmed. "Why didn't you tell me?"

"The alien is not programmed, as I am, against the taking of life. I think that the probe knows it is not functioning at maximum. If it knew that *you* knew that, I do not think that it would have any qualms about destroying you and the *Meriwether Lewis*. Its desire to fulfill its mission is very strong."

"If you're right, I can't take a chance on having it aboard the ship, Aristotle! I'll have to leave it here!"

"I regret to say that that is impossible!"

"Why? The probe is no longer connected to its armament on the exo-skeleton!"

"The probe has a powerful matter disrupting weapon housed in the brain core. If you make a move to leave it here, it will destroy us all. It is blind, relatively speaking, but it is still very, very dangerous. I am sorry, Tom. I could not tell you that I knew we were in grave danger from the moment you first saw the alien."

"We're in the hands of a homicidal maniac," said Tom. The full force of that knowledge was beginning to penetrate into his mind and with it, came fear.

"That is correct, Tom," said the robot.

Tom Swift burst through the hatch onto the bridge of the *Meriwether Lewis*. He had removed his helmet, but there had been no time to take off the rest of his suit. He leapt into the pilot's couch and yanked the crash harness into place. Ben, Anita, and Burt Foster were already strapped in, waiting anxiously. Aristotle had attached himself to the deck of the ship with his powerful electro-magnetic motorframe and was cradling the alien probe's brain core carefully.

"Get ready," shouted Tom. "I'm going to give the fusion drive its head! If I don't we're going to be cooked!"

Tom felt the ground under the ship begin to heave as he coaxed the powerful fusion drive into life.

It woke up with a roar and Tom suddenly felt as if he had an elephant sitting on his chest. The ship climbed rapidly into the black voice of space.

"I . . . I can't breathe!" croaked Foster.

"This is the *Daniel Boone* calling!" Rafe Barrot's voice sounded anxious. "We just picked you up on the screen and you're travelling like a bullet!"

Tom eased back on the fusion drive. He welcomed the sudden release of pressure. He heard the others gasp with relief.

"*Daniel Boone*," said Tom. "We're really glad to hear from you!"

"What happened to you? You know we lost you when you entered the flux tube. Did you find out what happened to Argus? Its signal died a while ago."

"Argus was destroyed in the eruption of a volcano on Io, Rafe. We just barely escaped from it." Tom wanted to tell Rafe Barrot all about finding the mad probe and about the Skree and the star drive, but he knew that Burt Foster had been right about one thing, at least. It *was* a top secret find and if the information from the probe fell into the wrong hands, it could destroy the Earth. He sighed wearily. "We're coming in, Captain. Have my father and a top security team standing by to

156

meet us at the hanger deck. I'll make a full report at that time."

There was a slight pause, then Rafe Barrot said, "Will do, Tom. Welcome back."

Tom wondered how much of a welcome they would get when he told them about the probe. And Foster? He would probably be court martialled for his handling of the *Meriwether Lewis*.

Yes, it would be *some* welcome. Tom stretched back in his pilot's couch and thought about what the rest of the alien's message might be. Maybe Foster *hadn't* been watching too many science fiction movies at all.

He would have to find out.

TOM SWIFT®
No. 1: THE CITY IN THE STARS
by Victor Appleton

A soundless explosion rocked the racing ship, shooting it out of control towards the Sun, and shearing off a chunk of white-hot metal that streaked down towards the floating space-colony, *New America*.

Tom Swift, son of the world famous scientist, was in desperate trouble. No space tug available—only a few hours air supply—and should he win through, what deadlier perils would he face with the knowledge he now held...

CITY IN THE STARS—The first in a series of great and dazzling space adventures starring Tom Swift.

0   552   52154   X

THE·ASTRONOMY QUIZ BOOK   Non-fiction
by Patrick Moore

What is the difference between a planet and a star?

How long will the Sun go on shining more or less unchanged?

Are comets members of the Solar System?

Is the Milky Way System an ordinary galaxy, or is there anything special about it?

The answers to these and many more fascinating astronomy questions are in this intriguing book—compiled by Patrick Moor, the most universally known figure in the world of astronomy.

0   552   54132   X   60p

If you would like to receive a newsletter telling you about our new children's books, fill in the coupon with your name and address and send it to:

Gillian Osband,

Transworld Publishers Ltd,

Century House,

61–63 Uxbridge Road, Ealing,

London, W5 5SA

_____

Name ....

Address ....

....

CHILDREN'S NEWSLETTER

All the books on the previous pages are available at your bookshop or can be ordered direct from Transworld Publishers Ltd., Cash Sales Dept. P.O. Box 11, Falmouth, Cornwall.

Please send full name and address together with cheque or postal order—no currency, and allow 40p per book to cover postage and packing (plus 18p each for additional copies).